LET ME LIST THE WAYS

Also by Sarah White

Our Broken Pieces

LET ME LIST THE WAYS

SARAH WHITE

HARPER TEEN
An Imprint of HarperCollinsPublishers

HarperTeen is an imprint of HarperCollins Publishers.

 For information address HarperCollins Children's Books, a division of HarperCollins Publishers, 195 Broadway, New York, NY 10007.
www.epicreads.com

Library of Congress Control Number: 2018933327
ISBN 978-0-06-247315-8

Typography by Torborg Davern
18 19 20 21 22 PC/LSCH 10 9 8 7 6 5 4 3 2 1
❖
First Edition

Katherine—

Always remember . . .

When you doubt yourself, you know your body better than most people will ever know theirs.

When you experience the pain that life can sometimes bring, you have danced for years with needles and lancets—this world's got nothing on you.

When you hear harsh words from ignorant people about your disease, remember you've spent years building up calluses against things that sting.

You are a fighter and a survivor. You have suited up to battle for your life everyday since before you had even spent a full year on this earth.

Keep your scars on the outside, Beautiful. I love you more than you'll ever know.

Love,

Aunt Sarah

Sierra Sandison—

I'll never forget the day you walked across the stage proudly wearing your insulin pump for the world to see. Hope can be a beautiful thing, and you filled my heart with hope for my niece. I still cry when I think about it. This is for you too.

I FELL IN love with Nolan Walker one hot afternoon on the playground of our small grade school. I have read that love feels like falling or flying, but on that Friday so many years ago, it was more like a bright light that descended upon the blacktop, lighting up everything in its path with a warm glow.

I'd been sick all week, running a low-grade fever and feeling flushed and shaky, but I hadn't wanted to miss a chance to play at recess with my best friend, which is how I found myself at the far edge of the blacktop playing King of the Court with Nolan. I was leaning up against the small brick wall when my world began to go black. It's odd that I didn't try to get help, to alert the teacher that something was wrong, but I didn't. Instead, as my vision began to tunnel, I looked over at Nolan. I watched Nolan as his eyes moved to mine and he let the small red rubber ball fly right past him in a move so uncharacteristically Nolan I felt my head tilt with curiosity. I saw his lips form my name, but the sound was drowned out by the growing ringing in my ears. Nolan caught me just as I tumbled to the ground.

I guess you could say that day was the scariest day of my life and one I would not soon forget. Hours later I'd sat in a too-large hospital bed in the local children's hospital as the doctor explained to my parents that I was a type 1 diabetic and would be insulin dependent for the rest of my life. I can remember the thoughts bouncing through my head as I stared at the brightly painted murals on the otherwise bleak walls: I was a sick child—and Nolan Walker had saved my life.

one

"NOLAN!" MY MOTHER screeched playfully as I heard the back door slam. I quickly smoothed my hair, which was pulled back into a ponytail, my long brown waves hanging in a messy tangle to the middle of my back. His feet fell heavy on our stairs as he trotted up to my room, my mom laughing from below.

"Sorry, Mrs. Clark!" he shouted down to her. "I didn't mean to startle you, I promise." I could hear the hidden smile in his words. He loved scaring my mom and she loved being a part of his little game. I wasn't the only Clark who seemed to love Nolan—just the only one who didn't love him like family.

The knob to my room spun and the door cracked open to reveal a smiling Nolan, his bright blue eyes laughing and his perfect lips curling up in a knowing smile. His hair was getting a little too long, but the way the deep brown strands nearly covered his forehead made me swoon a little. The feeling only intensified when he gave me a small wink.

I tossed a crumpled piece of paper at him but he quickly shut the door so that the paper bounced off the back of the white wood. I giggled when he quickly opened it again, peeking his face back into my room and offering me a scolding look.

"Are you cranky, Zie? I come bearing gifts." He slid inside the door and closed it behind him, something my parents would never object to. Nolan and I were around each other so much he was practically their other child.

I tossed my pencil down on my desk and used my feet to tip myself back onto the hind legs of the chair. "I don't get this. I hate that I have to memorize all this stuff when I'm going to forget it a few months later. Besides, when is anyone really going to grill me about the Louisiana Purchase?" I blew out a breath, my bangs scattering across my forehead. His low chuckle seemed to slide gently over my skin.

"I thought you and Regan were going to study together." He moved next to me and leaned back against my desk.

I squinted a bit as I looked up at him. "We might have

been kicked out of the library for being too loud yesterday."

Nolan laughed and shook his head. "You girls are trouble together." He spun my book around and glanced at the material I'd been trying to cram. "For the life of me I can't imagine what you would have been loud about. This is some pretty dry material."

"We didn't really get to the studying part of the session." I took my book back and returned it to its position in front of me. Quietly I mumbled, "We shouldn't have sat in the romance section."

Nolan quirked an eyebrow and leaned closer to hear me better. "I'm sorry. What does sitting in the romance section have to do with being loud?"

I rolled my eyes and gave him a little shove, pointing to my kit on the desk behind him. "Hand me that." I huffed out a breath. "We had every intention of studying, but there was this stack of old romance books sitting on the table calling our names." I glanced up at his face as he tried to contain his smile. "They were the cheesy ones with the man perched on something like a rock or a boat and some woman hanging from him." I mimicked the women's desperate poses.

"How did reading get you kicked out of a library?" he asked, laughing. He grabbed my kit off the edge of the desk and tossed it to me.

"You can't keep that gold to yourself!" I proclaimed in

earnest. "We took turns reading aloud the best scenes, which may or may not have been appropriate near the senior book club." I shrugged again.

He shook his head. "Leave it to you and Regan to corrupt the seniors." He glanced down at my history book again pointedly. "You're great at memorizing useless information, Zie. This test should be a piece of cake. Besides, I brought you a treat and some studying incentive." His eyes met mine, and that was all it took to make my stomach do a little flip. I wanted to brush his bangs out of his eyes but it seemed too intimate. "Of course, it's not as good as naked man chest, but it'll have to do."

I smiled at him as I slid the test strip into the meter. The day I found out I had type 1 diabetes, the doctor had explained that my pancreas didn't produce insulin, the hormone my cells needed to convert sugar into energy, but all I heard was that I was going to need to give myself shots and poke my own fingers multiple times a day for the rest of my life. When you're a child, there are very few things more terrifying than that. But the thing about living with an incurable condition is that you have no choice but to get used to it. My parents and I quickly had to learn how to test my blood sugar levels throughout the day, and how to figure out the correct doses of insulin to inject so that I stayed in an acceptable range. There was a lot of practicing, and Nolan had been there through all of it. He had been there in those first few days when my fingertips had turned purple from the pricks. He offered up his own so I could practice on him too. He had been there when, in sixth grade, I decided I didn't want to be diabetic anymore because it was too much work, only to be reminded very sternly by my endocrinologist that if I didn't check myself regularly and administer insulin when I needed it, I was at risk of some serious health issues, including everything from going blind to needing to have a limb amputated. Nolan had held me as I cried. And he was still there now, always keeping an eye out for the signs that my blood sugar had gotten too low or too high, and quietly supporting me every time I had a setback. I knew that kind of unconditional friendship wasn't easy to find, which was why it was such a simple decision for me to keep my feelings for Nolan secret. There was no way I could ever risk jeopardizing what we had.

Nolan glanced at my meter and made a small *tsk-tsk* with his mouth, but then shot me that devastating grin again. "Sixty-one, Sugar," he said, using his other nickname for me. "That's why you can't remember shit." He dug through his pocket and pulled out six Hershey's Kisses, to help me get my blood sugar back to the appropriate 90 to 120 range.

I shrugged and tossed a Kiss into my mouth, rolling up the small square of tinfoil and throwing it at him. "Well," he said, catching the foil and then flicking it off his palm for the perfect shot right to my forehead, "now that I'm here, I might as well help you study." He kicked off his shoes and lay back on my bed, making himself comfortable on my pillows. I watched him with mild amusement. He used to spend the night when we were younger and we'd both fit, but now his tall frame made his feet nearly dangle off the end, and the way his strong arms folded behind his head made the once-big bed seem child-sized. I giggled at the thought and he narrowed his eyes at me.

"What's so funny?"

I unwrapped another Kiss and put it on my tongue, taking a moment to enjoy the smooth flavor. Finally, around the melting lump of chocolate, I answered, "You look like Goldilocks in the baby bear's bed."

"Is that so?" he asked sarcastically. "I think this bed is 'just right.'" In one quick move he reached down and grabbed my ankle, pulling me off balance so that the front legs of the chair I was leaning back in slammed to the floor. That time he was the one laughing.

I moved to pinch him as he shut his eyes and rested, but he must have sensed what I had in mind because his hand shot out and captured my wrist. He cracked one eye open and gave me a heart-stopping smirk. "I know you better than you know yourself." As the words fell from his mouth, he yanked on my arm, pulling me from my chair, down onto the bed with him. I moved to get up but he just held me tighter, dramatically rubbing my bangs and the wispy hair that had escaped my elastic band into my face like a toddler would pet a puppy. "There, there, Sugar," he teased, and I laughed, giving up on trying to break free from his hold.

He finally released me and we both sat up, moving to the edge of my small bed so he could pull the huge textbook onto his lap. He flipped through the pages of my open notebook on my desk until he found a clean page and ripped it from the spiral binding, setting it on the pages of the textbook. Next he pulled a pen from the cup where I kept them and clicked its point down so he could write. "I think it's time for one of our lists," he said seriously, titling the page TOP TEN REASONS ZIE WILL NAIL THIS TEST.

I laughed. Even though I probably *wouldn't* nail the test, I knew I would save this one just like I had the hundred or so other ones we'd written over the course of our friendship.

Nolan turned to look at me, and for a second I thought he might say something serious because he pulled in a breath and gave me his full attention, but then no words came out.

"What?" I finally managed a whisper. His eyes left mine long enough to take in the rest of my face. His mouth opened to answer, but then quickly shut again.

His head shaking slightly, he smiled and whispered back, "Nothing."

two

THE NEXT MORNING the sun was up already as I made my way through the gate in our backyard. I smiled as my fingers pushed down the old dirty latch, securing it behind me. It used to be white, but over the years Nolan's and my hands, filthy from playing in the planters, had left their marks.

I took the two steps up to his back door and turned the knob, letting myself into his house.

"Hey, Mrs. Walker. Is he ready yet?" I asked as I stole a piece of bacon from the counter next to where she was cooking.

"I haven't seen him. I think he's still upstairs getting

dressed. Why don't you run on up there and tell him to get down here so he'll have time for breakfast before you leave? Seth and Gavin took off a few minutes ago." She took a break from the frying pan, wiping her hands on the small towel hanging from the stove. I nodded and set my backpack down on the kitchen counter. Nolan's younger brothers always rode their skateboards to school.

I took the stairs up to his room quickly, something I had done so many times I could have made it up them in my sleep. "Nolan?" I inquired as I opened his door.

"In here," he called from the small bathroom in his bedroom. "I didn't hear my alarm," he explained as he stepped out and gave me a smile. His wet hair hung down on his forehead and the smooth skin of his bare chest was red from where the hot water had assaulted it. I managed a nod, trying to act normal even though it felt like all the oxygen had been sucked from the room. After so many years of seeing Nolan as a friend, it still sometimes took me by surprise how attracted I was to him. I had always loved him, but in the last couple of years it became clear to me that I was also *in love* with him. I had noticed the little things at first, like the way my heart picked up its pace when he looked at a me a second too long, or the way my skin tingled with sensation if he whispered in my ear, the heat of his mouth so close to my neck. By the time I recognized what I felt for him, it was too late—I was completely in love. Luckily, he never seemed to notice.

"We have time." I tried to mentally shake off the sight of him in nothing but his towel. He nodded and pulled the bathroom door almost closed behind himself so he could get dressed. I watched the door for a few breaths, calming my heart before turning my attention to the bulletin board above his desk. Any tension from before vanished when I saw the nearly naked magazine girls again.

We'd been playing this game since we were about twelve. He'd hung up a few magazine pages of girls in bikinis or underwear, nothing too bad since usually they were from magazines his mother had at the house, maybe Victoria's Secret or some department store catalog. Once, while he'd left me alone in his room as he helped his dad with something in the garage, I had cut out very modest outfits for the women from some of the scraps of construction paper he had in his desk. It took him a few days to see my handiwork, but his reaction had been worth the wait. His brows had pinched together and he'd had to bring his face close to the images, as if he couldn't believe what he'd been seeing. Then the most beautiful laugh had burst from his chest and he couldn't get it to stop until long after his face had turned red and his eyes had watered.

As we grew older, he would replace the girls with newer

images, and I swear sometimes he picked the most provocative poses to make it more difficult for me to cover them. We never discussed it anymore; he would put the girls up one day and I would dress them another. He used to remove the little outfits I'd made, but lately he'd left them up, only taking down the pictures when a new catalog would arrive.

I slid the little drawer of his desk open and grabbed a sheet of printer paper and a pair of scissors. This model would be easy enough, standing straight at the end of the stage in nothing but a demi bra and small scrap of fabric covering her lady parts. I giggled a little as I cut out a turtleneck shirt and a pair of old-lady high-water trousers. I jumped slightly when his voice echoed from the bathroom.

"So my mom said that tomorrow is this month's game night with your parents. What are we watching while they get buzzed on chardonnay and play Spades?"

I quickly slapped some glue onto the back of the horrible outfit. "I'm not watching another superhero movie. I'm game for anything but that. There are only so many times I can watch men fighting in tights." I pressed the model's clothes onto the shiny surface of the magazine's pages, making a few trims where the sleeves were a bit long.

His chuckle filled the room. "I don't think you're supposed to be complaining about men in tights. How about a comedy, then?" I could hear the drawer in the bathroom open and the sound of him searching for something inside it. I pressed the trousers onto her long legs and stood back to admire my work.

"How about the new Channing Tatum movie? It's a comedy." I screwed the lid back onto the glue and tossed it into the drawer, then swiped the scraps of paper into the trash can beneath his desk.

"I thought you didn't want to see men in tights. I think his main outfit is a football uniform. I wouldn't want your eyes to suffer." The bathroom door opened, revealing Nolan in a pair of dark jeans that fell perfectly along the definition of his thighs, hanging a little low at his waist. His black T-shirt stretched across his arms and chest. He tossed his towel into the dirty clothes hamper by his bed and quirked an eyebrow, already expecting my smart-ass response.

"The tights rule only applies to average men—Channing's not average." I had my arms crossed against my chest and was trying to act casual as I used my body to block the modestly covered model from his line of sight.

"I stand corrected." He grabbed his backpack from the end of his bed and swung it onto his shoulders. Taking two small steps, he came to stand right in front of me. I could smell the fresh scent of his soap and see the smooth expanse of the skin on his chin where he'd shaved that morning. His fingers reached for the bottom of my shirt, his eyes falling to the hem as he tugged it lightly away from my stomach.

"It's a shame you didn't realize turtlenecks were the new thing." He shook his head a bit and then left me standing, unable to make my knees move as he touched the tip of my nose with his finger and headed downstairs to grab breakfast.

I didn't really understand how, after all the time that we'd spent together, Nolan could still take my breath away simply by standing close to me. I shook my head to clear it and made my way to the kitchen to find Nolan grabbing bacon without taking off his backpack. I pulled my phone from my pocket and saw that school started in ten minutes. He grabbed a bottled water from the fridge and tossed one to me also. "Did you eat breakfast?"

"Yes," I answered. "I got up early to finish studying." Slipping my backpack on, I tucked the water into the side pouch and headed to the kitchen door to follow him out. He nodded and moved down the steps. We made our way along the small side area between our houses before he unlatched a gate that led us to the front of the property.

He unlocked his truck from the passenger door like always, opening it as he took my backpack to toss into the bed. It was quickly turning to spring, so we both rolled down our windows as soon as he turned the key in the ignition. It was too early in the morning to have a conversation, so we just listened to the radio, Nolan's hands tapping out the beat of the song on the wheel.

Nolan's and my mornings had become a finely honed routine. Even on the days it was clear we were going to be late to our first classes, he still made sure to wait by my locker as I exchanged books and dropped my lunch off, and then I did the same for him.

"What article did you decide to write for this week's paper?" he asked as his strong fingers spun the dial of the combination lock, deftly stopping at their mark before spinning in the other direction. With the loud sound of metal clanking, his hand pulled the latch up and the door swung open. He moved his backpack to his front, leaving his history book in exchange for his English text.

"I decided to do the interview with students who have part-time jobs as refs for Little League sports teams. It should be a fun story to investigate. I have the feeling they're going to have plenty of stories about crazy parents getting upset about the calls they make." I smiled ruefully at Nolan but noticed that he had suddenly become distracted by the sight of a folded piece of paper lying on his books. My stomach dropped. Over the last few weeks, someone had been dropping off notes in Nolan's locker. Someone with feminine writing. Nolan had finally confessed to me that they were from Erin, a girl in the year below us who was not only a rising star on the volleyball team, but had that kind of wholesome, girl-next-door prettiness that I, Nolan's actual girl next door, must lack.

Nolan didn't notice my face fall as he smiled and grabbed the note before closing his locker. "Sounds like you've got another great story on your hands." His voice was peppy and I forced myself to smile back at him.

"Thanks, Romeo," I teased. He chuckled and patted his back pocket, where he'd tucked the note safely away.

"I'll give you all the juicy details at lunch," he said in a playful girl voice. Then when we got to my classroom door, he turned around and waved good-bye. I watched him walk down the hall, his fingers dipping into his pocket to retrieve the note.

My friend Evan bumped my shoulder gently with his and said, "Earth to Mackenzie." I pulled my eyes away from Nolan and gave Evan a playful shove back. I stepped farther into the classroom and sat down at my desk near the window. Sometimes I wished that correcting the feeling of jealousy were as easy as correcting my blood sugar on a good day, but it never would be.

three

"HOW DID YOU think the test went?" Regan asked me after we walked out of history together.

"Who knows?" I tucked a piece of hair behind my ear and closed my locker. "I hate essay tests. Why must they torture us like that?"

"They're brutal. I bet I failed and UC Santa Barbara is going to rescind my college acceptance." Regan was always worrying about failing tests even though she had maintained a perfect 4.0 average her entire high school career. "We're eating out on the grass today."

"Yeah, I got the text. The barbecue gets Declan every

time." I laughed as I finished zipping up my backpack. They start cooking lunch during fourth period, and Declan's classroom was right above the grills.

Regan and I slowly made our way through the crowd to her locker, stopping a few times to chat with friends and let them know where we'd be sitting. I leaned against the other lockers as she got herself organized. She grabbed her lunch and slammed the locker shut, turning the dial to clear the combo. We headed out to the big tree between the math and science buildings, where many of our friends were already sitting.

Nolan flopped down on the grass as I was opening the front pouch of my backpack to pull out the worn purple canvas bag that I always carry with me. He watched for a moment and then opened his lunch bag, pulling out his sandwich as I got everything ready. I swiped my finger with the small alcohol swab and put the test strip into the meter.

I glanced at Nolan as my number popped up on the screen a few seconds later. He reached inside his bag and pulled out a cold diet soda and a few Hershey's Kisses, which he set in front of me. I gave him a small smile in gratitude as I added a few more carbs to my total lunch count. There were days when my numbers were very high that he'd leave the Hershey's Kisses at the bottom of the bag. He didn't make a big deal over it or even let on at all that they were in there, just ignored them and shoved the entire bag into the trash when our time was over.

I wore my insulin pump in a soft belt around my waist, but I could control it from the meter I used to check my blood glucose. I gave myself enough insulin for the contents of my lunch and then tucked the meter back inside my kit and brought my sandwich to my mouth.

"I heard you have a secret admirer," Nisha sang playfully.

Nolan swallowed his bite and nodded. "She's not a secret." I noticed the way his lips curled up slightly as I tried to swallow down the tiny lump in my throat.

Nisha rolled her eyes. "Well, that takes the fun out of it."

"Sorry," Nolan replied. "You know I don't keep anything from Zie." He reached over and gave me a playful push.

I cocked an eyebrow as I told him, "And you should know I don't tell everyone your business."

"She's no fun either," Nisha complained. "I tried asking her about it all week. She won't spill the beans."

"Maybe because it's not your business," Declan pointed out as he tossed a Frito at her.

Nolan quickly jumped in. "Erin and I are just talking." He shrugged casually. "I don't think it's a big deal."

"Why doesn't she just text you?" Declan asked as he tipped the chip bag up and poured the rest into his mouth.

"I guess her mom reads everything she does on her phone." Nolan cracked open his soda and took a long sip.

"What is she writing that she doesn't want her mom to see? And do you write her back?" Nisha asked as she leaned in closer, her eyes wide with curiosity.

"Jesus, Nisha. Simmer down," Declan playfully scolded. I watched the interaction like a spectator at a tennis match. Declan and Nisha were legendary for getting into fights at the drop of a hat and then passionately making up five minutes later. Half our friend group thought they were going to get married and the other half was worried they would kill each other.

"I'm not much of a writer—I write her back, but my responses are more memos than novels," Nolan answered. "And she just writes random stuff." He looked over at me as if I could elaborate.

I shrugged at him, then set my sandwich down on my bag and pulled the water from my backpack. From what Nolan had told me, it sounded like she mostly wrote to him about what she did the day before, what her plans were for the weekend, and how much she was looking forward to the class they have together. It wasn't exactly scandalous, but it was enough to get the little green monster inside me growing and trying to scratch its way to the surface.

When the identity of the author was known to only

Nolan and me, it seemed contained. Now that our friends were finding out, it made it feel more real.

"Well, I think that sounds romantic," Regan said. "I would love it if some girl was leaving notes in my locker. It's like something that would happen fifty years ago."

Nolan pulled the note out of his pocket and flipped it between his fingers. Then he let it rest on his flat palm. Nisha reached for the small folded paper, but he curled his fingers around it and pulled his hand away before she could snatch it. "There's nothing in them you need to read." Nolan and Declan both chuckled at Nisha's squinted eyes. I tried to hide my amusement too. Nisha's eyes moved to mine immediately.

Nolan followed her gaze to my face and then shook his head. "She just proved she keeps all my secrets."

"But we have the Girl Code," Nisha proclaimed assuredly.

Nolan considered it for a moment but then tucked the note into the pocket of my jeans. "I'll take my chances. Now tell me about your game," he commanded right before shoving the rest of his sandwich in his mouth, the subject effectively changed.

Nisha perked right up, forgetting all about her quest for Nolan gossip. "We are going to kill them." Since our school's varsity softball team was undefeated this season, she was right to be confident.

"How's your pitch count?" Nolan rubbed his shoulder and I wondered if it was an unconscious movement or something he was aware he was doing. Was it hurting him again?

"I'm good. I probably won't pitch this game since Coach will want to use me against South."

I listened as the four of them talked about the season and the games that were coming up, but my thoughts kept drifting back to the letter in my pocket. I let my gaze drift across the field, taking in all the other students as they ate and talked in their groups. Before I knew it, the bell rang, letting us know it was time to pack up our lunches and get back to class.

Nisha and Declan headed off together in the direction of their shared fifth-period history class while Regan dashed off to math. Nolan turned to me with a smile and said, "Do you have a minute to read that letter for me? I want your advice."

"Sure," I answered, although I felt anything but sure.

I unfolded the letter, taking a minute to flatten it out and slow the jittery feeling that had taken over my stomach. I read her words on the paper, saying everything I wished I could say to him. Flirty little comments about how cute he was and how fun it was to sit by him in class. I hated the small heart she put before her signature and I hated that she was actually too nice of a girl to really hate at all. But it was the words at the bottom of the page that made my stomach turn. She asked why he and I had never dated. The thought of him writing an answer down, making it clear he had no interest in me, made my heart hurt, but I tried not to let it show.

As I folded the letter back up again, I could see the small tremble in my hand and wondered if it was from my blood sugar dropping or the letter I was holding. Nolan seemed to notice it too, and he took the note and handed me some cookies from his lunch. "Twelve each," he said automatically, to which I nodded and gratefully accepted them. Twelve meant the number of carbs each cookie contained. Nolan spoke my language.

"Should I take her out?" he asked.

I popped a cookie in my mouth to save myself from having to speak. Instead I nodded before reminding myself that I had to work on being a better friend when it came to this kind of stuff. I swallowed the cookie and forced myself to give him the advice I'd give a friend like Evan or Declan. "You should take her to the new restaurant that opened up outside the movie theater. I heard the food is pretty good and it would be easy to grab a bite to eat before a movie." There. I'd offered friendly advice. It almost killed me, but I threw it out there.

"Okay. I'll ask her out for Saturday since you and I have

a date planned for Friday night. Above-average men in football uniforms, right, Sugar?" A giggle bubbled up and I felt relieved that he wouldn't be missing our night together to go on a date with someone else.

"Five bucks says my mom gets drunk before nine thirty." It was a bet I couldn't lose. Nolan extended his hand to mine and gave it a little shake.

"It's a sucker's bet, but I'm in." The bell rang loud again and we both scrambled to our feet. We were late. We didn't have to separate again; our last three classes were together. If I didn't think about the weekend, I could almost pretend everything was normal. Almost.

four

NOLAN PAUSED THE movie and we listened to the screeching sound coming from downstairs. "What time is it?" he asked, reaching into his pocket for his cell phone.

"It can't even be nine yet," I laughed, turning my face so I could see the bright screen of his phone as he held it above us: 8:53. "That was a fast five bucks!" My mom's drunken laugh rang out again and both of us erupted in our own laughter. My mom was normally very serious. She worked at a bank in town part time and always followed every rule ever written. But once a month, when our parents got together for a game night, she and Nolan's mom would have a few glasses of wine and my mom would forget about all of them.

"Wait for it; my mom's own cackle isn't going to be far behind." His voice was laced with humor, and I bit my bottom lip, trying to hold in a laugh. Sure enough, within seconds we heard her laughter mix with my mom's, followed quickly by the deep male voices of our dads trying to warn the women they might want to slow down. They could warn all they wanted; our moms wouldn't listen, and they knew our dads enjoyed their buzz as much as they did.

"Should we go get a snack?" I asked, pushing myself up on my palms. Nolan's phone chimed. I moved off the bed and to my feet as he shifted and slid his phone into his pocket. He followed me down the stairs into the kitchen, and my dad rolled his eyes when he saw Nolan and me exchange knowing looks over the box of instant popcorn. "They haven't had that much," my dad said unconvincingly as I opened the plastic wrapping and popped the bag into the microwave.

"Just getting a snack," Nolan replied with equal conviction.

"Mackenzie, your hair is getting so long," Mrs. Walker said, resting her chin on her hand as if her head had suddenly grown too heavy to hold up on just her neck. "It's very pretty. You're growing up to be such a beautiful woman." She patted my mom's hand and gave her a smile.

"Thanks, Mrs. Walker," I said, turning red. I could hear

the quick pop of the popcorn in the microwave as all the eyes seemed to move to me.

"Nolan," she continued, "don't you think she's getting so beautiful? She's always been pretty, but there is just something about growing up that she seems to be doing so well." I grew redder as Nolan took me in. His eyes moved from my bare feet, slowly up my legs, and then up farther, until they met my own.

"Yeah, Mom, she's beautiful." He gave me a small smile before pulling the microwave door open and retrieving the bag of popcorn. I felt a totally different kind of warmth flood me as I replayed his words in my head, but almost immediately, any feelings of happiness were washed away by what my dad said next.

"You guys are practically siblings," he said, pulling a long sip from his beer. Nolan nudged me with his elbow and lifted his chin toward the stairs, signaling to me to head back to our movie. He seemed completely unbothered by what my dad had just said. As I waved to our parents and made my way up the stairs to my room, my heart felt heavy with the knowledge that everyone, including Nolan, saw us that way. Maybe it was because we had known each other for so long. I'd never regret our friendship and the years of happiness and support it had provided me, but if I was honest, in some small moments, I wished Nolan and I had met on different terms. Maybe if I had just sat next to him sometime in a high school class, our relationship could have been different.

I sat on the edge of my bed as Nolan opened the bag of popcorn and gave it a little shake to let the steam out as I quickly tested myself. He set the popcorn down on my desk and took a seat next to me.

"We should hurry up and start the movie again," he whispered playfully. "I don't want you to miss a minute of Channing in those tight pants, and I know you're going to be asleep long before it's over." I nodded and reached for the remote, drowning out the happy sound of our moms laughing with the soundtrack of the movie I knew I wouldn't be able to focus on. Instead I would be playing the scene downstairs over and over again in my head, trying to figure out whether he really meant it when he said I was beautiful, and wondering if I would ever be brave enough to just ask him.

five

IT WAS A beautiful day down at the Little League field. The sun was up, but the grass was still wet with morning dew when I pulled up behind the snack stand, careful not to park where the foul balls could hit my mom's car. I didn't see Eduardo yet, but the first game on the major field was not set to start for another thirty minutes. I grabbed my notebook and began to flip through the pages so I could find an empty one to take notes for my school paper assignment.

I flipped past the week's history notes and stopped when I found the familiar penmanship of my best friend. The list was titled TOP TEN REASONS NOLAN WILL NEVER

WEAR TIGHTS. His title alone already had me laughing, and I could only guess that he'd written it after I fell asleep last night. Unfortunately I didn't have time to read the list because Eduardo tapped on my window and I unlocked the doors so he could slip inside and answer my questions.

"Thanks for taking the time to do this," I told him.

"You're welcome." Eduardo closed his door and turned to me. I knew him from Nolan's baseball team.

"How long have you been a ref down here?"

"Two years," he answered. "I've played down here since T-ball." He pointed to the T-ball field with a smile on his face. "Nolan and I aged out together. Once we started at the high school, they asked if any of us wanted to ref. I didn't really have the free time in my schedule until last year."

"You must enjoy it if you came back for a second year."

"I do," he agreed.

"How are the parents? Do they ever give you a hard time?" I asked as I turned the page in my notebook to find a clean sheet.

Eduardo chuckled. "Most of them are pretty chill. I know some of the games can get intense. Not the younger ones, but the majors. One time I had a mom get so mad at me for not making a call in her son's favor that she threw her drink at me."

"Are you serious?" I asked, my pen scratching notes.

"I wish I wasn't." He shook his head. "She called me 'blind' and said that maybe the heat was getting to my head. I turned around and tried to nicely explain that her son had not thrown the ball to the catcher fast enough, but I never got a chance to finish my explanation. She practically ran down the bleachers and then threw her large drink at me."

"I can't even imagine that!" I told him.

"It was crazy. The best part was that the fence stopped most of the ice, and the soda fell short of me by about two feet. It took all I had to not tell her that she threw like her son—and that wouldn't have been a compliment."

"What happened after that?" I asked.

"I could have thrown her out for the rest of the game, but I didn't have to. Her husband was so embarrassed he told her she needed to go home and cool off. I think once she threw her drink she realized she'd gone too far." He laughed and shook his head in disbelief. "Are they crazy like that with you when you work in the snack bar?"

"No," I answered. "I get more attitude from younger kids. They always want more candy than they have money for." It usually only amounted to a quick math lesson and a few bratty back-talking sessions.

"Consider yourself lucky. Are you going to talk to Jude?" Eduardo asked. We watched as the coach of one of the teams pulled up beside us and started to unload his gear. Our interview was going to be over very soon.

"I am. I'm supposed to try and catch him at the end of the game he's working on the rookie field." We both looked up to the field, barely visible beyond the snack bar.

"He's got one of the most extreme stories I've ever heard. It will be a good one for your article," Eduardo said as he reached for the handle on the door.

"Thanks again for your time," I told him. "Good luck at your game."

"You're welcome and thank you. I'll see you later," he replied, correctly assuming I'd be at our school's baseball game this week. I hadn't missed one yet.

I glanced at the clock on my dashboard. I still had at least an hour before Jude would be finished and available to be interviewed. I grabbed the towel I'd brought from my back seat, knowing the benches would still be damp, and headed up the dirt walkway toward the rookie field. When I reached the fence, I could see Jude dressed in gray and black, crouched behind home plate. I stopped and waited there so I could watch him in action for a while as he called the pitches coming in. When the fourth ball flew over the dirt outside the plate, he motioned for the batter to take his base, and then his eyes found mine and I could see him smile at me through the black mask that protected his face. I gave him a small wave and headed to the stands.

I had known Jude for a while, though not very well. We had been in a class together last year and again this year, but this semester we had a table between us and most of our conversations didn't last longer than it took for us to walk into the classroom and find our seats. I had a newfound respect for him, though, as I watched how he refereed the game. I had been a fan of baseball for so long that I could see that Jude was doing a great job. No one was perfect, but his calls were fair. For the most part, Jude kept his attention on the game, not turning around to give any attention to the stands no mater what insults were thrown his way. I only saw him turn around twice, and that was when one father swore at the coach. Jude reminded him the players were children.

When the game was over, Jude climbed the bleachers and sat beside me. "Thanks for giving me some of your time on the weekend," I said as I patted the towel in invitation for him to sit.

"It's no problem," he said as he twisted off the top of a water bottle. He tipped it back and drank it down. The sun was up higher in the sky now and the day was warming up. I could see the sweat on his brow and the way his arms were a little red from the sun where they peeked out beneath his shirt. I'd never been that close to him before, and for the first time, I noticed just how dark his eyes were.

"Do you ever miss playing the game?" I asked him. I

remembered having seen him down there many times over the years, but he stopped playing when we started high school.

"Sometimes," he said with a shrug. "But I didn't love it like I think you should if you are going to play at the more advanced levels. I didn't want to give so much of my time to it. I'd rather spend that time surfing or just hanging out with my friends. It was fun when it was meant to be fun," he said pointedly. "When it became about winning the championship, it stopped being fun and became stressful."

"I could see that," I replied.

Jude bumped my shoulder with his own playfully. "So I heard you want to hear about the psycho parents." He laughed. "Have I got a story for you."

"I can't wait," I said as I got my notebook ready.

"You know those coaches that care so much about winning it's almost laughable?" he asked.

I nodded, remembering the crazy coaches I'd seen over the years while working the snack bar and watching Nolan's games. "Sure."

"Well, I was the umpire last year for a team in the playoffs. This coach was nuts. He wanted to win so much he was pulling out all these insane moves. It was so bad we had to get the board president to come down to the field with the rule book. Anyway, things were getting tense. The game was dragging on and the players were getting tired. His son was the catcher and the whole game came down to one play. I saw it very clearly. The runner slid beneath his glove and it wasn't a forced run so he was safe. Game over. They lost." Jude brought his hands in front of him and signaled the runner safe.

"Oh no," I said in anticipation of what might come next.

"He charged me," Jude said. "Not even kidding. This dude full-on charged me from his dugout."

"No way!"

"Dead serious. I couldn't believe it was happening. He took me down flat on my back and we slid for at least a foot in the dirt. He straddled me and actually got one punch in before the other coaches were able to pull him off me." Jude rubbed at his jaw as if remembering the hit.

"You're a teenager! He's an adult." I couldn't believe what I was hearing.

"And that's exactly why he got arrested and is now banned for life from ever setting foot down here again," he laughed. "Cops said we could get lawyers if we wanted and make a civil case out of it, but the guy felt bad when he calmed down and made a nice contribution to my college fund."

"What about his kid?" I asked. How embarrassing.

"I think he's happy," Jude said as he smiled warmly. "He

gets a coach that isn't as intense now. I see him down here all the time playing with his friends without his dad yelling at him from the field or the stands."

"Makes sense," I agreed. "I guess it's sort of a happy ending." I chuckle as I finish writing my notes.

"I'd take another punch to make sure that kid was happy. That's the way baseball is supposed to be. Fun, and played for the love of the game, not for the love of winning." Jude took another sip of his water. I'd never had a talk like this with him, and it was the first time I'd gotten to see his softer side. It was making it hard for me to keep my smile from growing larger the longer I sat beside him. He was cute and sweet. I wondered why I'd never really noticed that before.

"When does the article come out?" he asked.

"It will be out in the next edition," I told him.

"I look forward to reading it." He looked out at the field as he told me, "Your stories are always my favorite."

I felt my cheeks heat with his words, and inside my chest I felt both flattered and excited that he paid attention to my work in our school paper. "Thank you. For today and for reading my articles."

A car pulled up and the horn honked. Jude waved to the driver. "That's my ride." He turned to me as he stood up. "You're welcome. It was fun getting to spend time with you outside of class. Maybe we'll get to do this again sometime."

His expression was adorable, his lips lifting and his cheeks flushing slightly. He stepped down the bleachers and got into the waiting car. Once inside, he leaned over and tapped the horn again, waving one last time before the driver pulled out of the dirt parking lot and away from the cluster of Little League baseball fields.

Later that day, sitting at my desk, I heard the low rumble of Nolan's truck as he backed out of his driveway, leaving for his date with Erin. I told myself I wasn't going to look as he drove away. Instead, I stared at the black print against the worn cream paper of the novel open in front of me. I tried to read the sentence, but before I reached the end, I'd already forgotten the beginning. My feet pushed off the wall, letting my chair tip back on its hind legs, and I closed my eyes as I listened to the sound of his engine driving down the street. When the sound of his truck had faded into the distance, I let my chair fall back down and sat, staring at the wall in front of me, mentally starting the countdown until I would hear his truck return.

I knew that one day he would pull out of the driveway on a date with the girl who would be around forever. I wasn't ready for that yet and wasn't sure if I'd ever be. I never wanted anything to change our friendship, but I also knew that Nolan didn't do anything half-assed. He was the best friend anyone had ever had, and when he finally got serious with a girl, he'd be the most amazing boyfriend. How much time would that leave for me?

I knew one day I would find someone too. It was just hard to imagine what he might be like, because every time I tried, I could only ever think of Nolan. He'd need to be just like him. It was that knowledge that hurt the most. I already had the perfect guy; I just must not have been his perfect girl, because if I were, then he would've been out with me instead of some other girl.

Tomorrow I'd do the right thing and call Nolan to ask how his date went. Tonight, though, I was going to take a shower, put on my most comfortable pajamas, and binge-watch TV.

I must have fallen asleep after a few episodes because sometime just after eleven, I was jolted awake by the familiar sound of his truck pulling into his driveway. My eyes fluttered open and I held my breath as I waited to hear him go inside. His truck door shut, then the night returned to silence. I reached for my kit and pulled it onto the bed. I always tried to go to bed with my blood sugar a little high because I tended to drop sometime before morning. I was at seventy-three, just a bit lower than I'd like, so I took off my covers and made my way downstairs quietly.

I grabbed a small juice box from my shelf in the fridge

and pushed up to sit on the counter. I wouldn't drink much of it, just enough to raise my blood sugar to a level that would be safe to sleep. My phone vibrated on the counter beside me and my stomach did a fancy flip as Nolan's name appeared on the screen.

NOLAN: Are you awake?

MACKENZIE: Yes. Late night snack.

NOLAN: Let me in.

I let the cool juice roll across my tongue as I unlocked the kitchen door and cracked it open slightly. I could hear the latch on the small gate as he secured it behind himself, but it was too dark outside to see Nolan. Moving back to my position on the counter, I set down the juice and waited for him to come in.

Nolan pushed the door open just enough to slip inside and headed straight for the fridge. He took a juice from my shelf and then made his way over to where I was sitting and pushed himself up onto the counter beside me.

"How was your date?" The words felt like sand in my mouth. Nolan took a long sip of his juice before answering.

"It was nice. We went to the new restaurant you told me about." He smiled at me and took another sip from his straw. "It has a southern feel and they serve everything fried. We need to go sometime and get the mac and cheese. It came with like four different kinds of cheese and crumbs of some sort on top. It would totally be worth the burn." He lightly bumped my shoulder with his. Sometimes when I had to give myself a large bolus of insulin, it burned going in. I used to bounce up and down on the balls of my feet in a little dance when I was younger as it stung. Now that I was older, the burn was just something I tried to survive. Every so often, though, the reward was worth the burn.

"I'll have to try it sometime." I took one last sip from my juice box. The cold juice and the chill he'd brought inside made my skin break out in small bumps. Noticing, Nolan set down his juice and wrapped his arm around me, sliding his hand up and down my bare arms to warm my skin. I leaned into him, feeling myself melt into his side as he soothed the cold away. It felt natural to tip my head to rest on his shoulder and he instinctively tucked it beneath his chin, pulling me closer to his warmth.

I wondered for a minute if he'd held Erin. I wanted to know if he had the same instinct to care for her as he did for me, but saying her name and asking him about it would ruin this perfect moment.

"What are you thinking about?" he asked.

"Nothing," I replied, giving him back his answer from the other day. Nolan chuckled as I moved away.

"I better go to bed. I have five minutes before I miss curfew."

I wanted to stay there in the kitchen with him as long as possible, or at least for the next five minutes. Instead, I pulled my back straight and gave him a small nod as I slipped off the counter.

six

"WAKE UP."

I thought I was still dreaming when I heard Nolan's voice above me.

"Wake up. We're going on an adventure."

"It's too early for adventures." I tossed my pillow at him and tried to wrestle my tangled blankets over my head.

"No, it's not. But how about this for a deal—I'll check for you so you can lie there a minute longer." The metallic sound of a zipper quickly opening filled the air, followed by another as he unzipped the inner pouch and dug out an alcohol wipe. His fingers encircled my wrist as he flipped my hand up. Just because I was angry with him for waking me, I lowered every finger except for my middle one, holding it stiff for him to prick.

"Very funny, Zie," he laughed, wiping the cold alcohol swab across its tip. "Don't you want to hang out today? Maybe get a little sunshine?" The quick sting of the needle pierced my skin and I finally moved to sit up as he ran the testing strip beneath the drop of blood.

"It's not natural to be this chipper in the morning," I tried to say seriously, but I could feel my lips turning up slightly. He grinned back at me, his beautifully straight white teeth shining through as he held my finger to stop the blood.

"Fifty-eight," he said, his happy face falling into a more serious look. He set my kit back down on my desk and reached for his pocket. I flattened my palm and extended it above his lap, waiting for the shiny treats I knew would be placed there soon. Four silver Kisses were set on my waiting palm, and as I moved my hand back to begin unwrapping the chocolaty goodness, Nolan quickly unwrapped a fifth Kiss and moved it to my lips.

"If you wanted to give me a kiss, all you had to do was ask," I joked. I opened my mouth and let Nolan drop the Kiss onto my awaiting tongue. He immediately reached for one in my hand and began unwrapping it quickly.

"I don't ask for kisses, Sugar. In case you haven't noticed,

I give you all the Kisses I have." He touched the tip of my nose with his finger and leaned in as if to share a secret with me. "They take the bite out of your words when you're low."

"I know, I'm sorry," I mumbled around the gooey chocolate in my mouth. I tried to move to sit up a little higher so I could help take care of myself, but Nolan was already offering me another unwrapped piece.

"Some things are worth the burn." His attention moved from the candy to my eyes and I felt the stutter of my heart as his words fell over me. Hearing him say that I was worth the burn made my throat tighten with emotion. I moved my tongue through the thick chocolate, trying hard to find the words to tell him he was worth the burn too, but a playful Nolan shoved another two chocolates in, laughing as I started to drool.

"Get up and get ready, Zie. We are taking a little road trip." He stood up and clapped his hands together loudly. "I'll grab your beach towel."

"Fine. Can you grab me some more lancets from my box above the towels while you're at it? I'm almost out in my kit."

"Sure thing." He smiled wide now that I wasn't fighting his early wake-up call and impulsive day plans.

"Are you going to be gone long?" I heard my mom ask him from just outside my room.

"No, just a few hours," he answered. He stepped back

into my room and this time I noticed he was wearing board shorts and a vintage tee. I got up, opened the top drawer of my dresser, and turned to face him.

"What should I wear?" It may seem silly that I asked that instead of where we were going, but I trusted him. He did this often, planning some adventure for us to go on. I loved them, whether they were just to a new bookstore we hadn't visited yet or some new taco stand just because he knew I had a thing for them.

"Your purple bikini," he answered, springing onto my bed and grabbing the remote. When I just stood there, curious if we were headed to the beach or a friend's pool, he continued, "You know, the one with the little fringes." Nolan moved his hand in a weird motion, trying to show me where I'd find the fringes on my bikini top. I giggled and threw my towel at him.

"Thanks. I didn't know where the fringes were." I rolled my eyes. "Why that one?" I rested my hands on my hips, watching as he rolled my towel into a tight ball.

"Because I like it," he said, as if it was the most obvious answer, then he threw the towel back at me. "And because we are going to the beach," he finished as I spun around and retrieved the bikini from my top drawer.

I closed the door behind me and gave myself a small bolus of insulin since those Kisses had helped bring my blood sugar up. Not wanting to keep Nolan waiting long, I rushed through putting on my bikini and headed back out to my bedroom, holding my towel and pajamas. Tossing my pajamas into the dirty clothes hamper, I spun around, catching his gaze for a minute before he looked away. His eyes didn't linger or heat; they seem to bounce off my own before fixing on the show he'd been watching. I let myself stand for a minute at my dresser, turned away from him, and closed my eyes to focus on relaxing the painful clench of my insides.

It wasn't the first time I'd felt disappointed by his clear lack of interest in me romantically, but the deeper I fell in love with him, the more it seemed to hurt. When I could put a smile back on my face, I turned around. His attention was still on the T.V as I made my way around my bed to my closet to grab my sandals. I slipped the sundress in my hand over the bright purple material of the bikini and wiggled my toes beneath the small leather straps of the sandals now aligned at my feet.

"We'll drive through somewhere for breakfast," he said casually.

"Is it too early for tacos?"

"I don't think it could ever be too early for tacos. Especially not for a girl who eats Kisses for breakfast." The TV went black as he stood up and tossed the remote onto my bed. "Come on, Sugar."

After saying a quick good-bye to my mom, we made our way out to Nolan's car and headed toward our favorite Mexican restaurant. "Thank God, the sun is finally coming out again. I can't take that gloomy weather," Nolan said as he held his hand out his open window, palm up. He turned to me and smiled. Nolan had always been a summer person. He could only tolerate rainy days for so long before he was dying to get back out to the beach or back onto the baseball field beneath the bright rays of the big yellow orb he practically worshipped. I couldn't help but smile back.

"Do you remember that story Mr. Sax read to us the first day of our freshman year in Honors English? The one by Isaac Asimov."

"'Rain, Rain, Go Away.'" Nolan laughs. "That was such a twisted story. I remember thinking we were going to be in a boring class all year and was totally dreading it and then he introduced himself and opened with that crazy story. It was awesome!"

I laughed, softly remembering the way the class had been so quiet you could hear the swish of the page as Mr. Sax turned it as he read. The story is about a family that is made of sugar. They're invited to a carnival by their neighbors on a nice day. When it begins to rain, the neighbors watch as the family melts away. We had all been on the edges of our chairs, waiting to see why the family was acting so strangely.

Nolan and I went home and looked it up immediately, ordering more of his work on Amazon.

"Honestly, you would think they are . . . ," I started.

Nolan joined me and together we finished, ". . . made of sugar and afraid they would melt."

I looked at Nolan and noticed he was rubbing absently at his shoulder.

"Is it hurting?" I asked, trying to keep the alarm out of my voice.

"Not too bad. I think I might have slept on it wrong." He let his hand drift back onto the steering wheel, but it seemed like his face was pinched as if he was in pain.

"Maybe we should go back home and make an appointment with the doctor." He had a lot riding on his shoulder being in good enough shape to pitch his game.

"No. It's fine. It's just sore." I could see the hope in his eyes and maybe a shred of doubt. I wouldn't hold him to it because I knew he wanted his words to be true. He needed them to be. His scholarship to college depended on his ability to pitch for their team. There were many times over the years he'd let me pretend to be in a better place with my health than I really was; I'd give him this afternoon.

"Okay."

"If it's not better by tonight, I'll go on Monday," he promised.

I nodded and then put my feet up on his dashboard, hugging the bottom of my sundress around my thighs. "All right."

"But if you don't get your feet off my dash, you can walk home right now," he teased, reaching out with his bad arm and nudging my feet from the dashboard. We both laughed and the somber mood dissipated and our usual playful atmosphere returned.

"How are you going to boss me around when we're on separate campuses?"

He gave me a curious and worried look. "Are you having another 'dysgeographic' moment? I know you thought that the Gulf of Mexico was only in Mexico, so you might not realize this, but USC and UCLA are not impossible distances apart."

"Are you ever going to let me forget that?" I covered my face with my hands. That was the most embarrassing day ever. "It is named the Gulf of MEXICO," I said emphatically.

Nolan laughed so hard he could barely speak. "You were so sure."

"Why would I assume it stretches all the way to Florida?" I answered, as if he was the idiot instead of me.

"Makes perfect sense," he deadpanned. "And if the distance between our schools is too much, I'll just boss you around over the phone. Problem solved."

"I hope you aren't this mean to your new friends in college," I told him, crossing my arms over my chest in mock offense.

"It's okay if they don't like me. Why would I need any new friends when I've got you? After all, you've got all the answers I'll ever need." Nolan reached across the seat and nudged me playfully with his hand. I pretended to ignore him and looked out the window. Laughing, he announced, "Five Reasons You're Still Smarter Than I Am."

I giggled as I turned to look at him again. The moment he saw my smile, his shoulders relaxed. I loved making lists with him, all kinds of lists, but the lists he made about me were always my favorite.

seven

MY FEET SANK into the warm sand as Nolan and I made our way down to the shore. We spread out two towels and then left our bags on top of them. The heat from the sun kissed my shoulders as I slipped my cover-up off and dropped it into my oversized tote. Nolan held his hand out to me. "Give me your kit and I'll put it into the cooler bag I brought." I did as he asked and then stood, twisting myself slightly so I could reach the spot where my pump was connected to my body. I rotated it every three days, but I tried to keep it where any scarring would not be as noticeable. That's why that day it was just below the top of my bathing suit bottoms. I squeezed the small latches and pulled the connector needle from the cannula housing and slipped the disconnection cover in. He waited for me to wind the loose tubing around the pump and then took it from me to also place in the cooler. My pump was waterproof, but I hated taking chances with the salt water and sand.

I could hear the voices of a few of our friends approaching. When I stood up again, I took a minute to tug on my bottoms to make sure they covered the last site I had used, as it was still a bit bruised. You couldn't always see where my pump was last, but if you pressed just hard enough, you'd feel the bumps and dips from where it had been. Over the years, scar tissue had built up just beneath the surface.

"Zie, you're good," Nolan said quietly. I didn't really talk much anymore about how my disease made me feel different, but I still had a few tells. Leave it to my best friend to see one. He smiled at me, then waved at the group of approaching friends, shouting, "What's up?"

Regan, Nisha, and Declan made their way across the hot sand to our towels. We welcomed everyone with hugs or fist bumps and watched as our patch of sand grew into a small towel city. The girls quickly stripped down to their bathing suits and I felt a little jolt of envy seeing how they didn't have to worry about hiding a port beneath their suits. Snacks were secured in the cooler and sunscreen was applied. As the beach began to fill up with tourists and locals looking to soak up some of the early summer rays, we all settled into our spots on the towels to get some sun.

"Did you invite Henry?" Declan asked. We all turned and saw another group of kids making their way down the beach from the strand. I watched as Nolan's shoulders tensed when he saw his least favorite teammate. He and Henry were like oil and water, but they were forced to get along on an almost daily basis.

"This should be fun," I said under my breath, and Nolan bumped my shoulder with his. "Maybe they'll put their towels down somewhere else."

"I'll try to play nice."

I knew he would. It wasn't in his nature to ever give anyone a hard time. I was still watching him when his face lit up with a smile. I turned to see who had captured his attention. "Erin's here?" I asked.

Nolan turned to me with a bright smile. "Yeah. I thought it would be cool if she got to know everyone better. She's actually Henry's cousin. Isn't that nice?" The last words were said in a way that told me he thought it was anything but nice that his love interest had a direct connection to the guy he couldn't stand to be around.

"Lovely," I said flatly as I crossed my arms.

"Obviously I have the worst luck in the world. What are the chances they would run into each other here?" he asked as we watched Erin give Henry a hug and point to our group in a way that made it clear she was inviting Henry and his friends over to sit with us.

My towel was next to Nolan's, and by the time Erin made it to our group, the only place she could lay hers out was at the end of all the others. I didn't want to give up my space, but it seemed like the right thing to do. "Hey," I said as she finished applying some sort of lip gloss. "Maybe you and I should switch spots. I need to catch up with Nisha."

"Are you sure? That would be great." She slid her oversized glasses to the top of her head. "But only if it's not too much trouble. I don't want to put you out. You were here first." She looked sincere as she said it.

"It's not a problem." I smiled and then grabbed my towel and moved it down by Nisha's. That earned me a grin and conspiratorial wink from Nisha, who thought I was trying to play matchmaker to Nolan and Erin.

"So what do you think of Erin?" she asked when I flopped down next to her.

"She's nice." The thing was, she did seem nice. As much as I would have loved to have a concrete reason to not like her, she always came across as friendly. "Hey, did you see the last episode of *The Bachelor*?" I asked. My attempt to change the topic worked, and soon Nisha, Regan, and I had not only dissected all the drama that had happened on the group date on that week's episode, but had also analyzed *The Walking Dead*, and of course the latest HBO miniseries we were all hooked on. I promised not to give away the ending even though I'd read the book it was based on.

My stomach growled and Nisha laughed. "Let's get a snack. I'm starving too," she said. The three of us got up and headed down to the cooler and our bags that were stacked around the speaker and beneath the one sun umbrella Nisha had the foresight to bring. I reached for my kit while everyone else dived into the snacks they brought. As I was checking my blood sugar, I watched my friends eating and laughing together. It felt fun and perfect. I was going to miss days like this after we graduated.

After clipping my pump on quickly, I covered myself for what I'd chosen to eat, and then once the dose had been administered, I tucked my pump back in the cooler and put my kit away. Erin was just finishing a cookie by the time I came over and sat next to Nolan and opened my bag of mini cookies.

"Do you want one?" I asked Erin as she looked at my

snack. I'd calculated enough insulin for the whole thing, but I'd just eat something else if she wanted a few. I didn't want to be rude.

"No. Sorry," she said, looking away. "I just thought diabetics weren't supposed to eat sugar."

I actually got that all the time. I shook my head. "When you eat sugar, your pancreas makes insulin. When I eat sugar, I just have to give myself the insulin. Obviously I can't go crazy and eat my weight in sugary products, but I can have some cookies here and there. I need to sometimes if my blood sugar is low."

When Nolan was finished with his cookie, he brushed his hands on his board shorts and jumped up. He offered his hand to Erin and pulled her up too. Since I was still eating my snack, I waved off his offer to join them. I watched as he and Erin headed down to the water, a few of my other friends in tow. Nisha waited around for me, sitting down beside me on the towel and watching as our group dipped their feet in the waves at the shoreline.

"Do you think Henry and Nolan will learn to get along for the sake of Erin?" Nisha asked with a hint of mischief in her voice. We looked down to the shoreline at our friends splashing each other as the waves rolled in. As if perfectly on cue, Henry cocked his arm back and unleashed a huge wave of salt water right in Nolan's eyes as he was trying to help Erin up. I could tell even from our distance that Nolan gave Henry a sharp look as he wiped the water from his face.

"No," I answered with a sigh. "I think that ship has sailed." I crumpled up my empty snack sack and shoved it into the small bag we were keeping our trash in. "Come on. Let's go down there before someone gets themselves drowned."

"What's the fun in that?" Nisha asked with a laugh. We both got up and headed for the waves and our friends.

By the time lunch came around, my shoulders were a bit red and my fingers were pruned from spending so much time in the water. We all headed up to our towels and decided we'd pack up our stuff and head to a pizza shop on the pier. In a rush, I clipped my pump onto my bathing suit bottoms to save the time of unwrapping the tubing before reattaching it to the site on my skin, and then I pulled my sundress over my head.

"Do you ever get tired of wearing that thing?" Henry asked, his eyes on the lump at my side where my dress had caught up on my pump. "It's probably hard to hide all the time." It wasn't even his words that stung, it was the look on his face as he said them. I was used to people being curious. I was used to people not always being educated about my disease, but the only thing that hurt was when they were disgusted. There was nothing disgusting about it, but I couldn't help but feel shame anyway.

I was flustered as I tried to think of my response. My hands immediately tugged at my dress and then fidgeted with my pump to try to move it to somewhere more inconspicuous. "No. She gets tired of the ignorant assholes who ask stupid questions." Nolan's voice wasn't harsh, but it was laced with a warning that was very clear.

Henry laughed as he shook his head. He knew better than to challenge Nolan, especially in front of all of us. He told me, "Sorry. I didn't mean anything by it. I was just curious."

"It's fine," I muttered under my breath.

"It's not," Nolan told me quietly as we walked up to the pizza place.

"I think a lot of people wonder about it."

"Wondering is different than being disgusted. He's an idiot." Nolan bumped my shoulder with his and smiled. I tried to smile back, but it fell flat.

"Some days it doesn't bother me." I told him honestly. "And some days it feels really unfair."

"I get it." And I knew he did. He didn't need to say another word.

I promised myself I wouldn't let it ruin the rest of my

day. I tried not to focus on where my pump was in relation to my clothing, or if anyone was noticing it, but Henry had turned a spotlight on something that I already felt self-conscious about when I was in my bathing suit. It made me hate Henry a little more than I already did.

eight

IT HAD ONLY been a week since we'd all spent a day together at the beach, but the weather was beautiful and it was easy to be reminded of the warm sand and refreshing waves. "I still think we should have gone to the beach today," Regan said again.

She, Nisha, and I were around the table drinking chocolate shakes. The movie we'd just gotten out of had been funny, and the perfect way to spend a Saturday morning.

"I got enough sun last weekend," Nisha said. "Besides, we're going to the beach tonight."

"A bonfire isn't the same thing as lying out," Regan said, rolling her eyes.

"Are you going to meet up with Charli tonight?" Nisha asked mischievously.

I looked to Regan and watched as her cheeks flushed red. She'd had a crush on Charli for the entire year. Last weekend they were supposed to meet up for coffee but Charli had to cancel last minute when she had to spend time with her dad on a weekend that was typically her mom's. "Maybe," Regan answered with a shrug. She quickly sucked her straw into her mouth so she couldn't answer a follow-up question. It didn't deter Nisha.

"So are you going to meet up with her for dinner, then?" Nisha's spoon froze over her shake; a large drop of whipped cream fell from it and landed with a splat back into her cup.

Regan shook her head. "No," she answered. "Charli has some very severe food allergies. She has to carry an EpiPen. She said it's really hard to eat out. She's allergic to soy, which is pretty much in everything. Lots of places don't even know they're cooking with it so it can be very dangerous. She told me she has to call ahead and get the ingredients to every menu item." Regan's eyes met mine. "It reminded me of you, Mackenzie. She said people often tell her that things are gluten-free like that should be enough for her. They don't take the time to learn about her condition. I know people do that to you too."

"I just wish I had a dollar for every time someone told me if I ate healthier or exercised more it would cure me. They think I caused this disease. And only half of them listen to me when I point out that there is a difference between type 1 and type 2. I can imagine how frustrating Charli finds it, trying to explain her allergies to other people," I said.

Regan gave me a sympathetic look. "I told her I wanted to spend time with her. It doesn't matter what we do. She has to eat and I'm happy to be a part of that no matter what it looks like. I don't want her to be ashamed or embarrassed."

"She's lucky," I told Regan. "I'd like to say I'd never think twice about checking my blood sugar in front of a date, but it would be a lie."

Nisha dropped her spoon back into her shake. "I don't know why you do that to yourself," she said lovingly. "If we don't care when you check yourself in front of us, you must realize that plenty of other people won't care either."

"I know," I answered. "It's just getting over that first step with new people. I also wonder if they'll notice the way it's changed my body." I held out my hand; my cold fingers were wet from holding my frosty glass. The calluses on my fingers were easy to see.

Nisha leaned forward in her seat and made a big show

over squinting her eyes like she couldn't see anything until Regan and I were laughing. "But seriously," Nisha said, taking my fingers between hers, "we all have scars. No one makes it through this life without them. You just wear more of yours on the outside."

"True story," Regan said, nodding in solidarity. We were quiet for a minute and I thought about Charli and how brave she was to share everything with Regan.

"Maybe you could take her to that coffee shop that has the old books and overstuffed couches," I offered. "I saw on their sign once that you are allowed to bring in your own drink as long as someone in your party is a paying customer."

"Great idea!" Regan practically squealed.

"No problem," I told her. "Looks like it's just you and me going to the bonfire," I told Nisha.

"Girls' night out," Nisha sang as she shimmied in her seat.

It could get chilly on the beach at night, so I opted for my dark skinny jeans and a white tank top. I opened the small jewelry box on my dresser to find a necklace, settling on the new necklace my mom had bought me for Christmas. It was a thin silver chain with an antique-looking key hanging from it. I put it over my head and watched as the beautifully intricate key hung over my shirt.

I heard Nisha pull up outside and quickly grabbed my kit from my desk and shoved it into a small purse that matched my outfit. I took off down the stairs, excited to be going out.

"Bye, Mom!"

"Bye. Have fun and be home by midnight!"

"You look so good," I said as I slid into Nisha's small Honda, reaching across the center of her car and wrapping my arms around her neck as she struggled against her seat belt to return the hug.

"You too. I called Kara and she said everyone is already down there." She looked behind us and pulled the car out onto the road. We blared the music and left the windows down as we sang our hearts out. It felt good to be with her. I was happy and the night was young.

The parking lot near the beach and the row of beach-front homes was packed with cars when we finally arrived. We got out of the car and began to make our way down to the fire, which we could see burning in the distance. Loud music was booming across the dark beach, and in addition to the large group of kids we could see around the fire, small groups had broken off and were scattered all along the shore. Nisha had made the poor choice of wearing wedge sandals, and even though she was having trouble walking across the beach, she refused to admit defeat and take them off. She gripped tightly to my arm and I tried to support her as she wobbled along the loose sand.

Nisha pointed to a group of people to the left of the fire and was about to say something when her foot slid to the edge of her wedge and her ankle buckled, causing her to tumble and to take me with her. One second we were on our feet, the next we were sprawled out on the sand, my purse thrown somewhere when I flailed to try to save us.

"Oh my God!" Nisha spat some sand from her mouth and tried hard to find my hand. "I'm so sorry!" We both started laughing. I tried hard to contain my giggles, but the two of us together seemed to feed off each other's energy and we couldn't stop.

I felt a hand wrap around my bicep and pull up, trying to steady me and get me back on my feet. My first instinct was to pull away, the euphoric high of our giggle party dissipating quickly when I couldn't make out who had their hand on me. "Mackenzie, Nisha. Are you guys okay?" Declan's voice sounded worried and I let my arm relax, feeling the easy smile return to my face. I brushed the sand from my arms and legs as quickly as possible, starting to giggle again slightly as Nisha attempted to regain her composure and get to her feet.

"I'm fine." I almost forgot for that moment that we were in public and tons of our peers were just beyond the darkness. I looked up to where the music was playing and saw the figures moving in the glow of the fire on the beach in front of us, and I remembered exactly what was happening. "Go on, we'll be okay."

"I'm not so sure about that," Nisha joked as she wobbled a little more before reaching down and pulling off the stupid wedges.

"You girls are trouble together," Declan teased as he motioned for Nisha to hand him her wedges. She complied immediately, and then he bent down and she climbed onto his back. I loved seeing the two of them together. He used the flashlight on his cell phone to help me find my purse.

"Is this where the party's at?" a voice asked from behind us. Declan turned the beam of light in his direction. Bennet, a boy from my math class, tugged his girlfriend over to where we were standing.

"It's always a party where these two are at." Declan grunted as he bounced Nisha up higher on his back. We headed over to where the fire was burning and I quickly greeted my friends with hugs. I wouldn't say that I was one of the most popular kids at school, but I was one of the most liked. I made it a point to be friendly to everyone.

"Mackenzie, come sit by us." Maria called me over to where she and a few of my other friends were sitting. We had been in the same friend group for a while, but Maria and

I really bonded over the last couple of years by working the snack bar down at the Little League field together, on those days when parents would pay someone to work their shift so they could watch the game instead. It was a win-win situation since we were always around anyway, me because of Nolan and she because of her older brothers.

"What's up?" I asked as I sat down beside her.

"We heard that Nolan and Erin are going out. Is it true?" she whispered loudly so I could hear her over the music.

"They're spending time together and talking a lot." I shrugged. I wasn't really sure if they had a title yet. I hated when people asked me things about him. It always felt like I was violating his trust to talk about him, but at the same time I didn't think he'd mind since he wasn't really hiding the fact that he was into Erin. As if just thinking about him could make him appear, I saw the two of them emerge from the darkness and step into the light of the glowing fire.

Nolan waved and Erin gave me a friendly smile. They were soon swallowed up by a group of friends and I went back to chatting with Maria. Every once in a while I'd find myself looking for him. Old habit, I guess.

nine

THE FIRE WAS warm and the sound of people talking and laughing filled in all the space around me as I sat on a log at the edge of the flames. Alcohol had made an appearance about an hour ago, and it was clear some people were partaking a bit more than others.

"Right, Mackenzie?" asked Jude. He was in dark jeans and a zipped-up sweatshirt, not the black-and-gray gear I'd seen him in during our interview last weekend. I suddenly became aware of the fact that I had been so busy watching one guy by the cooler of beers belt out an eighties power ballad that I had no idea what they were talking about.

"Sorry, it's hard to hear over the music." It was a lame excuse considering they didn't really even have to raise their voices to talk to each other, but he let it slide and started over.

"I was telling them we had third-period science together last year and the teacher was so boring half the class would fall asleep." He smiled at me.

"Right. It was awful." I turned my body into the conversation and tried to pay better attention. Jude and I hadn't talked a lot in that class either but when we did he was nice, always joking around and getting into trouble.

"This kid in the class, I think his name was Ronny or something, had this calculator watch and he could control the DVD player with it. He used to rewind or fast-forward any movie we watched in class."

I laughed and added, "Our teacher never figured it out. Ronny did that all year, and each time Mr. Miller would try to send out for help making it work right. When the maintenance guy would come, Ronny wouldn't mess with it, so they must have thought Mr. Miller was crazy." Jude was nodding at my words, and we all laughed when he made this overdramatic flustered face that very strongly resembled the poor teacher's.

Everyone else had their own horror stories of terrible teachers too, and soon we were in a heated debate over whether it was worse to have a class with Ms. Baker, who thought it would be a good idea to only speak in Spanish every Friday even though she taught math, or Mr. Simon, who would make everyone read the textbook while he napped in the corner. It was one of those perfect nights where everyone was relaxed and having fun. When the other people who were sitting on the log with Jude and me left to go dance or refill their drinks, leaving just us to sit together, Jude turned to me and said, "So, I think this is only the second time I've seen you without Nolan."

"I mean, we're good friends. But we don't do *everything* attached at the hip," I said, smiling. I began to feel a small chill and ran my hands up and down my arms to warm up.

"That's cool." His smile widened slightly. "Nisha is in my history class. She was telling me about your love for *The Bachelor*."

"Guilty pleasure."

"My sister watches it every season. I might have caught an episode or two." He chuckled, and I knew immediately he was confessing to watching far more than just a few. "I balance it all out by watching *The Walking Dead*."

"Sometimes I secretly wish I could combine the two," I confessed.

"That's brilliant."

"When the girls start whining, I'm on my couch wishing that somewhere in the background you'd see the outline of a corpse slowly approaching. I think some of the women are so busy worrying about themselves they wouldn't even hear the groans."

Jude laughed and nodded. "It would be amazing. She'd just be sitting there complaining about how some other girl had a better date than she did and then this rotting corpse would be coming up behind her." He tipped his head to the side like the undead and mimicked a low groan.

I laughed. "Right. We wouldn't have to wait for the bachelor to vote the women off. Just let them get eliminated by the horde of zombies. I swear sometimes these men pick the most annoying women just to drive us viewers crazy."

"I agree. Zombies attacking would definitely make the show something the whole family could enjoy."

"Would you ever go on the show?" I asked him.

"As the bachelor?" He chuckled, his hand on his chest and his head already shaking. "No. It's not my thing. Way too much drama. I like to keep things simple. I don't think I could juggle all those dates and I wouldn't want to have to send people home."

"I think that would be hard too," I agreed.

"And . . . ," he said, his face pinching slightly as if he was trying to decide if he should share the next thought, "I know this sounds terrible, but I'd have to be attracted to the girls. I'm not saying it's all about looks, but I'd want to be into her. What if I wasn't really into any of the girls they picked for me?"

"I wonder about that too. Maybe the girls grow on the guy." I shrugged.

"Yeah, that's the exact story I'd want to tell my grandkids. 'I wasn't really into your grandma, but she grew on me.'"

His words caused a burst of laughter to explode from my chest. "Good point. Better that the spark is there immediately," I agreed.

"I think it's better to just meet someone the old-fashioned way." He smiled at me and my stomach flipped. He was really sweet, and now I knew he was funny and just as silly as I was at times.

"Ah," I said with an exaggerated nod. "Online."

"Or maybe in an ad," he said, playing along. "Single male looking for female who enjoys zombie shows . . ."

"Hates whining," I added.

"Doesn't judge men who watch TV shows geared for the female demographic and"—he glanced around before swinging his arms wide—"enjoys sitting on the beach at night with friends."

"She sounds amazing," I said with confidence.

"I think so too." His answer made my heart race in my chest. "So do you think she'd give me her phone number?"

■ ■ ■

Twenty minutes later, Jude's ride came over to let him know he needed to leave. Jude waved good-bye, having not only gotten my number but also my promise that we would get together soon. I couldn't stop smiling as I made my way back to the bigger circle to find Nisha. Nolan found me first. "Zie, can we talk for a minute?"

"Sure. What is it?"

His mouth opened to say something, but then my necklace must have caught his eye. His hand reached out and took my necklace in his fingers. He gave it a little tug, bringing me closer to his face. "This is new," he said in a low voice, mostly to himself. He wasn't acting right. Something seemed off about his behavior.

"Nolan, what's going . . ."

"You look really pretty, Zie." His hand released my necklace and reached for a thick curl of hair that was resting against my shoulder. He gave it a small tug and took another step closer. I could smell the faint hint of alcohol on his breath.

"Nolan, are you drunk?"

"Probably." He laughed softly. He let go of my hair and wiped his hand down over his face. "Do you like him?" he asked. My eyebrows drew together. Liked who? He rolled his eyes. "Jude. Do you like Jude?"

"He's nice." I couldn't help the smile that tipped my lips up. My cheeks flushed and then my skin chilled as the cold night air hit it. He handed me his beer and I thought he wanted me to take a sip so I brought it to my lips, but he quickly pulled my hand away from my mouth.

"No, don't drink. I'm just taking off my hoodie." He fumbled with the bottom of it, and now I was beginning to really see the signs of his inebriation. His shirt moved up with his sweatshirt as he lifted it over his head. I laughed again, watching him struggle a little to get himself untangled.

"Nolan." I barely said his name when his finger came up to my lips and silenced them. When he was sure I wasn't going to protest, he pulled the sweatshirt over my head and I helped put my arms through the sleeves. His hands reached behind my neck and gathered my hair, pulling it loose from the fabric and twisting it over my shoulder.

"Jude's a nice guy," he said, finally releasing my hair when he got to the ends. "He'd be a good one to pick." He reached down and grabbed his beer. "The Kisses are in the front pocket, Sugar." He tapped me on my nose and then rested his arm across my shoulders, pulling me into his side. I dug my hands into the pocket and unwrapped the first chocolate. I'd check my sugar when I got closer to the fire. "Come sit by me and Erin for a while."

I looked up just in time to see the look on Erin's face. She was hurt to see Nolan's arm around me, and that made me feel guilty. I pulled away from him, and when his gaze met mine, I looked over at her so he'd know why I'd done it. He recovered quickly, moving over to her and taking a seat right beside her. I sat across from them; the fire was small by that point and I could easily participate in the conversation all around me.

I tried not to look at their hands clasped together and the way he kept leaning in to whisper something in her ear. I wasn't sure if the feeling in my chest was jealousy or disappointment. Maybe the word for it would be longing.

ten

NISHA DROPPED ME off just before midnight. I made my way up to my porch and let myself into the house. It was quiet inside; my parents were already asleep upstairs. My phone vibrated in my pocket and I was expecting a text from Nisha wanting to make sure I had made it inside okay, but it was from Jude.

JUDE: I had fun talking to you tonight.

ME: I had fun talking to you too.

JUDE: Are you doing anything next Friday? I'd like to take you out somewhere.

I slowly sat down on the couch in my dark living room and reread his text. Jude was a really nice guy, and I had had fun with him. I leaned back and let out a big breath. It made me anxious to think about going out with someone, but I knew that it was time I took that step. If Nolan thought Jude was a good guy and I'd had a great time talking to him, then what more did I need to know before accepting his offer? Maybe he was the answer to finally getting past this silly crush I had on my best friend.

ME: I'd like that.

JUDE: Awesome! I'll see you at school and we can hammer out the details.

ME: Ok. Good night.

JUDE: Good night.

My thumbs hovered over the dark keyboard of my phone, itching to cancel and just forget about the whole thing. I was eighteen and had never even kissed a boy. The more I thought about Friday, the more it felt like going out with Jude was like jumping into the deep end of the pool without ever having swum at all. I forced myself to put my phone down, though, and tried to distract my attention by pulling out my kit and checking my sugar. It was almost perfect, which would be wonderful if I wasn't about to go to bed for the night. I wandered into the kitchen to find a snack.

Nighttime snacks were a little harder to choose. I would have gone with a bowl of cereal, but the milk and sugary flakes are hard to measure perfectly and I was convinced that there were somehow these sneaky carbs that hid in there and would make me go high all night. I decided to slice an apple and eat a few pieces without giving myself any insulin so my blood sugar wouldn't drop too low while I slept. I was two small slices in when my phone vibrated again.

NOLAN: Are you up?

ME: Kitchen.

NOLAN: I'll be over in ten.

ME: Ok.

I unlocked the back door just as I heard a car pull up in his driveway. I stood almost completely still, as if they could see through the walls and find me in the kitchen with half an apple slice hanging from my mouth. The car wasn't there long before pulling away and I waited for Nolan to come over, but he didn't. I watched the clock on my phone, wondering if maybe he'd forgotten about me.

Finally, I decided he was just drunk and I needed to head to bed. I was reaching for the lock on the back door when Nolan pushed the door open and peeked inside. His hair was wet from a shower and he smelled fresh and clean.

"Hey." He stepped inside and closed the door behind him.

"Hey." I moved out of the way and leaned back against the kitchen counter.

"We had a class with Jude last year, right? Science? And you have a class with him this year too?" He turned to look at me, and his dark lashes framed his big eyes that I knew by heart were blue even though it was impossible to make out the color in the faint light from the back porch. I wasn't sure why we were talking about Jude. I wondered if this was what it felt like when I asked him about the girls he talked to. I'd done it so many times over the years that it felt odd to be on the other end of the conversation.

I nodded and looked down at my feet. "He asked me out for Friday." The words seemed to rush from my mouth on a burst of air, and I waited for them to settle between us. I had never shied away from telling Nolan about crushes I'd had, mostly on movie stars, but this felt different. This was the first time I had ever agreed to go out with someone before.

Nolan didn't move. He didn't even seem to breathe, just stood like a statue, watching the side of my face as I stared down at my feet. I wanted him to say something, and I could swear I heard the loud tick of minutes as he stood silent. Finally he smiled and shifted his weight. "That's great. I think it's good you're going out, Zie."

I didn't know that it was possible to feel relief and disappointment at the same time until that moment. On the one hand, my conversation with Jude hadn't miraculously erased my feelings for Nolan, so it stung to see that he was happy I was going out with someone else. On the other, I had felt a real connection with Jude when we were talking earlier, and I was glad that my best friend approved of him. Still, the whole conversation didn't quite feel right. I wasn't sure if it was because we'd never had one like it before, or if I was just nervous and overthinking everything.

I cleared my throat and stood up, turning so I could face him. "How much have you had to drink tonight?" It was weird being in that position, the one where I was taking care of him while he was impaired instead of him taking care of me. I never drank, but there had been a handful of times when my blood sugar dropped very low so fast I needed his help. I'd been diabetic for so long sometimes I suffered from hypoglycemic unawareness and I wouldn't realize my blood sugar was dropping until it was already very low.

"Not too much." He stood too, pushing himself off the counter. "I guess I should go home. It's getting late." He tapped my nose with his finger. "Although I like that you're taking care of me." He motioned between us with his finger.

I couldn't help a small chuckle. "I was just about to say I

was enjoying this." I used his trademark move, tapping my finger on his nose this time.

"Are you nervous about going on a date?" he asked.

"A little, I guess. I don't even know what I'm supposed to do." I brushed my bangs from my eyes and sighed.

"What do you mean?" When I didn't answer right away, he reached over and gave my hair a small tug just like when we were little and I didn't do what he wanted. I laughed and swatted at his hand.

With a big yawn, I answered, "I haven't even kissed a boy, Nolan."

"Why not?" I was aware he already knew that I had no experience in anything *boy*, but we never talked about my love life so I guess it was a fair question for him to ask. I shifted a little uncomfortably.

"I guess I just had an idea in my head of what it would be like and reality hasn't measured up yet." It was the truth. I may have left the part out where I admitted that I pictured my first kiss being with him, but he was drunk, not me. I knew better than to say something like that and make everything awkward between us. Instead I just pushed his shoulder and told him, "You better go home. You're about to miss curfew."

eleven

BY WEDNESDAY AFTERNOON I couldn't think of my date with Jude without becoming a ball of nerves. Every time we passed in the halls, Jude would give me an adorable smile, and we had been texting pretty constantly, talking about everything from the road trip he was planning with his cousin this summer to how I should do a piece for the school paper about the mystery meat our cafeteria used (I was firmly against that idea). But as easy as it was talking to him over text, I was still terrified that I would do something horribly embarrassing on our date. And, though I hated to admit it, I was worried that my feelings for Nolan would get in the way.

I was sitting in sixth period, watching Mrs. Parker as she drew some sort of crazy diagram on the board at the front of the class and running through possible topics of conversation in case Jude and I ran out of things to say to each other on Friday, when my phone vibrated in my pocket.

I quickly stopped the buzzing and tucked the phone beneath the desk to hide it from her view. It didn't really matter; she was known for getting so wrapped up in her lectures that she never paid much attention to any of the students.

NOLAN: Are you coming to my game tonight?
ME: I'm sitting right next to you. Why are we texting?
NOLAN: Because Fiona is a nosy chick who will listen to our deepest secrets.

I glanced at him and he raised an eyebrow. From just over his shoulder I saw Fiona craning her neck to see what we were doing. I bit back a smile and quickly tapped out a response.

ME: You have deep secrets I don't know about?
NOLAN: Just one. Answer my question.
ME: Yes. I'll be at your game. My parents are coming.
NOLAN: Sweet. Do you think her neck hurts yet?

I glanced up again, and sure enough she was trying so hard to see what he was typing that she looked like she was about to fall out of her seat.

ME: For sure.

NOLAN: Erin is going too. Maybe you guys could sit together. It'll be the first one she's gone to.

I froze for a second, unsure how to respond. As a best friend, I should be totally excited about an open invitation to make friends with his girlfriend . . . wait, was she his girlfriend?

ME: You guys getting pretty serious?

NOLAN: Define serious.

ME: Never mind. Not my business.

NOLAN: Everything's your business. Define serious.

ME: I don't even know. You're talking to the girl who's going on her first date Friday.

When a response didn't come right away, I chanced a glance at him. He was staring down at his phone, thumbs hovering over the screen. Finally, three tiny dots appeared, chasing each other in our text thread, letting me know he was typing a response.

NOLAN: First date. I never really thought about that. Crazy. Anyway, back to the definition.

ME: Crazy indeed. The definition of serious? I don't know. Would you say that she's your girlfriend?

NOLAN: No. She isn't my girlfriend. We haven't updated social media statuses or anything like that.

ME: So you define serious as a public announcement on social media?

His response took a while. I stole a glance at him as the teacher lectured. He stared down at his phone as if he was deep in thought. Finally the conversation bubble popped up on my screen.

NOLAN: The social media status update is probably a result of a conversation in the relationship. Erin and I have not agreed to be exclusive. I don't ask her who she's talking to and I don't assume because she and I are spending time together I'm not free to talk to other girls if I wanted to.

ME: You aren't bringing other girls to your baseball games.

Maybe they weren't saying it, but his behavior was definitely showing me that he was getting more serious about her.

NOLAN: True. I guess I hadn't really thought about it like that.

I moved to tuck my phone away, thinking our conversation was over, but it buzzed in my hand.

NOLAN: Are you excited about your date with Jude?

My heart began to race as I read the words on my screen. So many things were changing and I couldn't help but think it was all happening too fast. My stomach felt unsettled and I noticed a headache starting to build behind my eyes.

ME: Yes. I'm nervous too. I'm worried I'll be awkward.
NOLAN: You're not awkward and you guys looked like you were having a good time together at the bonfire.

I read his words, and while I knew he was being supportive and saying all the right things, I felt irritable. I couldn't explain to him why I was so nervous about the date, and my feelings for Nolan seemed almost burdensome as I tried to make sense of all my emotions. The teacher's voice droned on in the background and I gave up, typing out a quick response and resting my chin on my hand when my headache grew more insistent.

ME: I guess you're right.

The bell rang loud and startled me a little in my seat. I gathered up my notes, which were actually just a few doodles I'd made at the beginning of the lecture. Shoving everything into my backpack, I waited for Nolan to make his way over to me. He wiped a drop of sweat from my forehead with his thumb and then reached for my bag. "You don't look so good."

"Thanks, Nolan," I replied sarcastically, and handed him my bag.

"I bet it was that stupid pasta you ate for lunch. You know those carbs sneak up on you. Want to check yourself before we head out to my truck?" He set my bag on the desk and waited for me to respond. He knew better than to be pushy with me. I could take a little nudge, but pushing me to check myself never ended well, especially when my blood sugar was high.

"I don't really feel so good," I admitted. My skin grew warmer suddenly, as if just his mentioning my blood sugar had made it skyrocket. "I think I should check it now." He only nodded and unzipped my bag to retrieve my kit. The kids in the class paid no attention to us, packing up their belongings and rushing for the door. I was moving slowly, so Nolan helped open the strips container and held it so I could pull one out. I slipped it into the meter.

I wiped the alcohol over my fingertip. The lancet pierced my skin and a drop of blood pooled easily on the tip. I closed my eyes for a second, the headache pounding now and the nausea building in my gut. When I opened them I looked at Nolan; his brows were pinched in worry. "Zie, you're four thirty. It says you don't have any insulin on board."

"Okay," I said, twisting my hair up off my neck to cool myself down. Lunch was a few hours ago, and while I'd covered myself for what I thought the pasta contained, I was off, and now none of the insulin I'd given myself was still in my bloodstream. Nolan's fingers moved quickly, setting up the amount of insulin I'd need to get my number back down.

"Is this okay?" he asked, showing me what the pump recommended. I nodded and he quickly pressed the button to administer the insulin.

Nolan tucked my supplies back into my kit and zipped it up in my backpack. Neither of us said anything about what had just happened. As much as it sucked when my blood sugar got out of whack, and as infrequently as it happened now, we had both had enough experience dealing with situations like this that it usually didn't faze us.

We walked out of the classroom and down to our lockers and then out to the parking lot. At his truck, he opened the passenger door, and I climbed inside while he threw our bags into the back. I wasn't sure how to bring the topic up again, but with the fog clearing in my head I realized I wasn't sure what I was supposed to call Erin if my parents wanted me to introduce her to them. It would be so awkward. I rolled down my window so the air could help cool my hot skin and decided I needed to bring the topic back up.

"So should I introduce Erin to my parents as your friend?" My hair whipped around my face and I struggled to tuck it back behind my ears. My hair ties were all in my backpack in the bed of the truck. Nolan chuckled at me and lifted the folded-down seat between us, producing a hair tie from a small compartment.

"You left it in here after the beach." He handed it to me and put his hand back on the steering wheel. "Maybe it would be best just to leave a title out of it."

"Sure, because that's not awkward and our moms will totally just roll with it," I returned sarcastically with a pointed look and a small chuckle.

He thought about it for a minute as we drove along, finally drawing in a big breath and shrugging. "Just say she's my friend. It's the truth. I didn't give her any kind of title when I introduced her to my parents."

"You don't think that will cause trouble between you guys or make her think I'm trying to put her in that category?" I twisted my hair up and out of my face. I could watch him then as he kept his eyes on the road, rubbing his free hand over his lips a few times.

"Why would it cause a problem between you and her?" He looked at me for a second and then back to the road.

"If I was sort of serious with you," I started, and he laughed at my choice of words, "and your best girl friend introduced me as just a friend, I might think she was not being respectful of what we were."

"Maybe you're right." His voice was contemplative, and he turned to look at me when we reached a red light. I wasn't expecting such a quick agreement with my line of thinking, so it took me by surprise. We held each other's gaze for a few seconds, but so many thoughts were racing through my head I had to look away.

He'd already introduced her to his parents and had invited her to his baseball game. Those weren't steps he'd taken with a girl in a long time. It was starting to have all the potential of a serious relationship, even without the title. I couldn't figure out what was holding him back. I knew he'd mentioned the freedom to talk to other girls, but he wasn't doing that, so why was that important to him? Finally

I decided I'd just ask the question I couldn't figure out the answer to on my own.

"Why isn't she your girlfriend?"

He reached down and pushed the blinker lever so that the cab filled with a ticking sound. He turned to face me as we waited for the light to change. I could tell he was holding something back and anger began to spread through me. I thought we weren't supposed to have secrets from each other, but he was keeping something from me. I knew I was being a hypocrite because I had my secret as well, but I still felt justified in being seriously annoyed with his little secret.

Finally, when I thought I'd have to pull it out of him, his mouth flattened out and his eyes took on a serious cast. "Because she doesn't like how close I am to you."

"What did she say? Did she ask you to stop being my friend?" Could she really think we'd stop being friends?

"She asked me what exactly my relationship with you meant." We pulled into his driveway and he killed the engine, our windows rolling up as we unfastened our seat belts.

"And?" I asked, turning my body completely so I could face him. I don't think I'd ever wanted to hear an answer that bad in my life.

"I told her, 'Everything.'" His smile stayed on his lips for the briefest of seconds and then dipped into something much more morose. My heart, which had been bursting with excitement and validation, suddenly stuttered under the expression on his face.

"She still wanted to be with you, then, even if we're going to stay as close?"

He shrugged a little and then opened his door, stepping down to the ground before staring back up at me.

"Then she asked me what your and my romantic relationship was." I waited at the edge of my seat, praying that something had changed and he'd told her so. I wanted him to say that he told her he liked me and that's why they weren't going to be serious, but I knew something wasn't adding up. He couldn't have said such a thing and have her still wanting to be with him in some way. I reached for the handle of my door but kept my eyes focused on his.

"What did you say?" I asked in a voice much more steady than I was feeling inside, especially since I couldn't read the expression on his face.

He gave a little shrug. "I told her it's nothing. We're only friends."

twelve

I HEARD MY mom yelp downstairs and shook my head, knowing that Nolan had gotten her again. It only took a few seconds for him to get up the stairs and knock on my door. It cracked open at his first rap, and he pushed it open a little wider, peeking inside. "Zie?"

"What if I wasn't dressed?" I teased. He slipped inside and moved to sit on my bed. I loved seeing him in his baseball uniform. The dark blue jersey and tight gray pants perfectly showcased his defined muscles. No girl could argue that baseball pants weren't one of the top ten inventions in men's fashion. In a move that made my heart beat quickly, he twisted his baseball cap backward so he could see me better. I watched his bicep flex and the muscles of his forearm bulge slightly with the movement.

"You would never change without locking your door. You're the most modest girl I know." He leaned back on the palms of his hands and looked me in the eyes. He was right. I'd never change if there was a possibility that someone might see me.

"Whatever. One day you're going to swing that door open and I'm going to be standing in here in just my underwear and then we will never be able to look at each other again." I took a few steps into my bathroom and grabbed my brush from the drawer. My parents weren't leaving for the game for another hour, but I wanted to get ready early so I could ride with Nolan.

"If I could still look at you after that awful neon phase you went through, our friendship could survive anything." He moved from the bed and past me into the bathroom, turning and lifting himself so that he was sitting on the counter beside me. I rolled my eyes and ran the brush through my hair.

"All right. I can agree the neon wasn't my best look. But I'd like to remind you our friendship has also survived the 'deep V' season." I pretend to shiver. "Not cute, Nolan."

"I was a misguided youth. No one told me a deep V neckline was best on a muscular chest and not on a prepubescent boy. Tragic . . . and yet not as terrible to look at as mismatched animal prints." He shook his head and I began to gather my hair into a ponytail as I laughed.

"Those were bad," I agreed. He reached out and tickled me while I had my hands tangled in my hair. "Stop!" I laughed and struggled to keep a hold of my ponytail while he continued to attack. It didn't matter which way I weaved, he followed along and tickled my sides until I finally gave up and let my hair go.

I slapped at his hands and he jumped off the counter and stood behind me so that I could see his face in the mirror. "Here, I bet I could do this faster." He began to gather my hair in his hands. This I had to see. Everything with him was always a race. It had been that way since we were little. Anything I could do, he'd try to do faster. But he was about to be wrong. I watched him in the mirror as he focused hard on getting my hair to stay in one place. I couldn't help but giggle at how terrible he was at it.

After a few minutes of struggling, he had most of my strands in his hand, secured at the nape of my head. I held up a hair tie and quirked an eyebrow, knowing that getting it wrapped around was the hardest part. He seemed to accept the challenge as he took it from me and went to work again. The first time through was more successful than I thought it would be, but getting the full length through the tie again was much harder, and even though he tried his best and tugged the hair tighter, half the ponytail went through and the other half tangled itself into some sort of half loop.

I laughed out loud as he made a frustrated face. His eyes shot up to meet mine in the mirror. "Are you laughing at me?" I immediately flattened out my lips and shook my head quickly, trying to act serious, but when the strands that had only been modestly secured slid from the tie and the whole ponytail unraveled, I couldn't help the smile that spread across my face.

When we were little, he used to hate when he couldn't do something as well as I could. Those times were rare, but his frustration each time made them seem so much more monumental. He put his hands in my hair and messed up what was left of the epic failure of a ponytail. I was laughing hard at this point, bent over trying to escape his playful hands. He moved them down to tickle my sides again before wrapping them around my waist and lifting me off my feet.

I tried to grab on to the counter, but it was too late. He swung me around easily and walked a few steps to toss me onto my bed. I turned over quickly so I could block his next attempt to tickle me. From that angle I could see his bright smile as he reached for my arms. In a split second, they were pinned above my head, and even though I tried to move my legs and break free, it didn't faze him and he just straddled my body and held me down tighter. I tried to talk but I couldn't through the laughing.

His hands moved my hands closer until he was able to hold both my small wrists in one hand. "Don't!" I managed, but he was already taunting me with his free hand, threatening to tickle my side again. I squirmed beneath him, but he just moved with me and ran his hand down my side. We were both laughing; his hand felt firm on my side as he first squeezed and then quickly moved his fingers to tickle very effectively. I took a deep breath and tried hard to sound serious when I said, "It's not funny." He made a very serious face and stopped for just a second.

"You're right," he agreed, and I nodded, lifting up against his hold on my wrists, but not being successful at breaking free. "It's hilarious!" His hand was back at my side with a vengeance. As I wiggled and bucked beneath him, he leaned forward to keep his hold on my arms. Our faces were so close I couldn't even see his entire expression. I was only able to focus on his features one at a time. His lips were curled up, his cheeks flushed red with exertion, but what made my stomach clench tightly was looking into his eyes. They were crinkled at the side with his smile, but as soon as our gazes locked, the skin around them smoothed out and he looked straight into mine.

We didn't move for what felt like forever. His one hand was still holding my wrists above my head and the other rested flat against my side. I was amazed at how quickly the sensation of being tickled was drowned out by the electric feeling of his heavy, warm palm touching my bare skin where my shirt had ridden up. I could hear my throbbing pulse in my ears and knew my face had to be flushed from the laughter and struggle of a few minutes ago. Our breaths were in sync.

I felt my chest rising and falling with my labored breathing and became acutely aware of the way it brushed against his each time we inhaled. I would only have to lift my lips slightly to meet his, but the fear of rejection kept my head planted firmly to my mattress. I wanted that kiss so badly it hurt physically, but it wasn't right, and it would be a second of satisfaction for years of pain that would follow. Instead, I closed my eyes, unable to look into his gorgeous blue ones.

He released my wrists and sat up taller. I wasn't brave enough to open my eyes until I felt the tip of his finger touch the tip of my nose in his trademark move. "Finish getting ready, Sugar. I'm going to be late." He moved quickly back to his feet and stepped away from the bed, offering me his hand to help me up. I took it because, let's be honest, I always would.

"I'm not responsible for your childishness," I said playfully as I was lifted to my feet. I moved back toward my bathroom, pausing to look over my shoulder and stuck my tongue out at him. I tied my hair up and threw the brush back into the drawer. Nolan sat back down on my bed and waited as I grabbed his hooded sweater out of my closet. It still smelled like him, and I fought the desire to bring it up to my nose and sniff it. I'd had it since the bonfire and would be a big liar if I didn't admit that I'd been thinking of a million reasons to keep it. I knew rationally that it wouldn't smell like him forever. That thought was what helped me toss it to him.

"Thanks," he said, grabbing it as it sailed in the air.

"You're welcome. Thanks for letting me use it." He just nodded at me and folded it up while I searched for another sweater in my closet. I pulled an old gray one from the hanger and slipped my feet into a pair of sneakers. I tried to fit my kit inside the front pocket of the hoodie, but it was too big.

"I'll put it in my bag. Just let me know if you need it during my game. I can get it to you easy if we're batting and if not, I can get it to you between innings." He was truly a great friend.

"Thanks." He twisted his cap forward and lifted his chin toward my door, letting me know we needed to get going. I followed him down the stairs and we gave my mom a hug good-bye before climbing up into his truck.

He turned down the volume on the stereo that was automatically blasting every time we got into his truck. "I'm picking up Erin. I hope you don't mind." His words felt heavy; I had to quickly remember to smile and act casual so the pure weight of them didn't flatten out my lips.

"Of course I don't mind."

He drove through the intersection and switched lanes to make a right turn. I stared ahead at the city in front of us. I wondered if he laughed with her the way we laughed together. Did he let himself into her room like he did to mine? Suddenly all the things I loved about my relationship with him felt like the very things that kept us friends instead of more. I wanted everything with him. I wanted the casual comfort we had around each other—but also the kisses he had with her. I wanted the laughter and intoxicating joy I felt when I was with him—but also wanted to give him the feeling of butterflies and desire like he got with her. But mostly, I wanted him to be a part of my life forever because of all the things I knew for certain in my life, the truth that was more true than any other was that I couldn't be Zie without Nolan. So I accepted that I'd be the friend he'd always find comfort in, the one he'd laugh and experience joy with, and someone else would get his kisses and give him butterflies, because having Nolan as a friend was a thousand times better than not having Nolan at all.

thirteen

NOLAN PULLED UP in front of Erin's house and parked. I wasn't sure what I was supposed to do next. I thought it might be odd if we both went up to her door, but it also didn't seem right that I stay in the car. I thought waiting in the truck might make her think I was being standoffish. In the end, I didn't have to make a decision because she was out her front door before he even had a chance to get out of his seat.

I opened my door and jumped out, giving her a small hug when she reached the truck. I knew the right thing to do was to give her the front seat next to Nolan, but it sure felt odd when I climbed into the backseat. Nolan gave her a quick kiss and then turned to me and gave me a tight smile. "Thanks for picking me up," Erin said as she buckled her seat belt.

"Of course. I thought it might be nice if you had someone to sit with." He motioned over his shoulder to me in the back. "Zie's family is coming in a little bit and they're super cool. You should have about forty-five minutes before the game starts so I thought you could hang out together." Nolan's eyes met mine in the rearview mirror. I could see that he needed me to be okay with spending time with her. It felt like he was asking permission, and that didn't help the guilt that was already moving into my heart.

"It'll be fun." I gave him a little nod and then busied myself looking out the window. I wondered what she and I would talk about once he was busy with the team. I knew she was going to want to talk about him and I worried it was going to be awkward for me. I was worried about that line that I had trouble navigating. Would I say too much? I was grateful for the music that filled the cab and made conversation unnecessary. We finally pulled up to the school. I unclasped my seat belt and practically leaped from the truck.

Nolan grabbed his bat bag out of the bed of the truck and took Erin's hand. She grinned with what could only be described as pure joy and my heart stung with envy for what she had with him. Despite what Nolan had said earlier about not being serious with Erin, he clearly cared about her.

When we got to the stands, he gave her another quick kiss. I tried to look out across the field at anything other than what was happening right beside me. When he stepped into my line of sight, I made sure to put on a smile. He touched my nose and gave me a tight smile. "If you need your kit or anything, just tell me."

"I'll be fine," I assured him quickly. I had always appreciated how conscientious Nolan was about my diabetes, but in that moment, it made me feel embarrassed that he was worried about me because of my health.

I sat down on the bleachers and watched him walk away before turning my attention to Erin. "So, Nolan says this is your first game?"

"Yeah, I've never been before. Thanks for sitting with me." She sounded very sincere. She'd always been nice to me and we'd had a great time at the beach, but there was a little part of me that wished we hadn't gotten along so well. I wanted a reason to not have to accept her. I was being evil and hoping that she said or did something unforgivable so that I didn't have to sit right by her and watch as she fell for my best friend.

"You're welcome." There was a lull in the conversation as I scrambled to think of something else to say. "So, um, you and Nolan have a class together?"

"Chemistry. First period. Mr. Torrez." She made a disgusted face and I laughed. He was an awful teacher who insisted on keeping every window and door closed, even when the classroom got so stuffy you thought you'd suffocate.

"Sorry about that," I said.

"It's okay. I guess it's worth it to get to sit by Nolan." That lull returned with a vengeance and brought his friend awkward with him.

I could see Nolan looking over at us between pitches as he warmed up his arm. When we were younger I'd catch for him. We would pretend it was the World Series and the last batter was up. I remembered the way he'd pretend to watch the imaginary runner on first before pulling his leg up to gain the momentum to send the ball flying over the home plate we had drawn in the dirt. I'd call them strikes, even when they were balls, and then we'd jump up and down and cheer as if he'd just shut the batter out.

The bleachers began to fill with a few people here and there. "So you guys have been friends for a long time?" Erin asked.

"Since we were kids. We live next door to each other." I held on tight to the wood plank below me and leaned forward a little. "Our parents are friends too."

"That's nice," she replied. "I know this is a little weird;

I'm not really sure what kind of relationship you have. I hope you don't think I'm trying to take too much of his time or anything."

"We're just friends." It came out a lot stronger than I thought it would. I hoped it would be enough to convince her.

She laughed without humor and turned her head in my direction. "What the two of you have together isn't 'just friends.' Everyone can see it except maybe the two of you. It's like you're in a relationship but without the fun stuff." I wanted to argue with her that we had a lot of fun together, but I of course knew that wasn't what she was referring to.

"I know our friendship is unique. A lot of people just don't understand it." I met her eyes.

"Doesn't it make it hard for you to date people? I saw you with Jude on the beach. Does he care that you and Nolan are so close?" She wasn't being snarky or mean, just curious. It was almost as if I could see the wheels turning behind her eyes, trying to figure out how all the pieces of our puzzles could possibly fit together.

"Jude knows about our friendship." I could only imagine how it must feel from her side. If I was dating Nolan I'd be afraid to lose him too. She just didn't see that I wasn't really competition. Saying Jude's name made me realize that he shouldn't be competing with Nolan either. "You don't have anything to worry about. Our relationship isn't like that." I could see the relief in her face as she nodded at me and then looked out to find Nolan again.

"I think it would be nice if the four of us hung out. Maybe we could double date or something?" Ugh, that sounded horrible. I hated the quick car ride there—how was I going to survive a whole night of watching the hand-holding and kisses?

"Sure. That sounds fun." I totally lied.

Once we got that out of the way, we fell into a friendly conversation again. I'd never had the chance to speak with her alone before, but it was clear that if we had, we would have figured out that we were actually quite similar in many ways. She told me about her family and how much she hated some of her classes. We both loved country music and we were both only children. I think in another life she and I could have been great friends. Maybe we would be eventually. This pining in my heart for Nolan would have to come to an end. I'd have to let him go so I could watch him be happy with someone else without hurting inside.

Henry's parents arrived and Erin waved to them. They quickly waved back, but made no move to come greet her or invite her over to where they were sitting. They took their seats far away from where we were and turned their attention to the field quickly. It was hard to believe they were her aunt and uncle, but the feud between Nolan's family and Henry's ran deep, and I counted as Nolan's family in their absence.

A few minutes before the game started, I spotted my and Nolan's parents making their way across the field from the parking lot. Seth and Gavin, his brothers, were carrying food from the local burger place and trying to trip each other as they headed toward the stands. I giggled as they stumbled and recovered. I waved everyone over to where we were sitting. I felt Erin grow stiff beside me and I knew she must have been nervous about being near his family.

I, on the other hand, felt at ease with all of them. They were practically my own. My mom climbed up and sat behind me. I touched Erin's shoulder. "Mom, this is Erin. Erin, this is my mom, Julia." In the end I had gone with not giving her a title at all and hoping no one would ask for one.

"Nice to meet you." Erin smiled up at her and gave a little wave.

"This is my dad, Sean." She gave a small wave to him as well, and then Nolan's mom moved in to sit next to my mom. I shook my head a little in warning. My mom rolled her eyes.

"We are going to be quiet," my mom insisted, and Mrs. Walker nodded in agreement and zipped her lips with the invisible zipper. It lasted for maybe two minutes.

"Nolan! Strike him out!" Mrs. Walker screamed above

me as Nolan stepped up to pitch.

"Get 'em, Nolan!" my mom joined in. Nolan smiled from beneath his cap. He said he hated their screeching, but I knew deep down it meant a lot to him to have everyone's support.

Seth climbed up the bleachers and moved to sit next to me. He looked a lot like his big brother, but had lighter hair and darker eyes. He wrapped his arm around my shoulders and gave me a kiss on the cheek. He always teased Nolan about making me his girlfriend. He loved to see Nolan get his feathers all ruffled and go into protection mode. From the field I saw Nolan scowl at Seth, but Seth just flipped him the bird and nuzzled up a little closer. Gavin sat down in front of me and began shoveling fries into his mouth.

I didn't have any siblings, but those boys were close enough. I tangled my fingers into Gavin's shaggy hair and messed it up. He slapped my hand away and tossed a fry at my forehead. "Stop it," our moms said in complete unison. See, just like siblings.

"Are you coming to my game on Saturday?" Gavin said around a mouthful of fries.

"Of course she is," Seth answered. "Nolan already said they'd be there." Seth and Gavin were closer together than Gavin and Nolan. The Walkers had lost a baby a few years after Nolan was born, and it took them a while to move on from that loss. Gavin was fourteen now and Seth was on the newer side of thirteen.

"If Nolan said we are going, then I guess we'll be there." It wasn't unusual for Nolan to assume we would be hanging out together on a Saturday. Actually, that statement could apply to any day of the week. We were together all the time and rarely ran plans past each other.

The loud slap of a fastball hitting the catcher's glove caught our attention, and Nolan's eyes met mine for a second before returning to the ball in the catcher's hand. My heart jumped from the sound. I caught the glare reflecting from Erin's phone in the corner of my eye and turned to see what she was doing. She had both elbows on her knees and was focusing all of her attention on the shiny screen in front of her. She typed out a few texts in rapid succession and then opened up the Facebook app and scrolled through a few posts.

"Want some fries?" Gavin asked, holding the greasy bag out in front of me. I reached inside and took a handful. Seth pulled a small container of ranch dressing from his bag and handed it to me. I quickly covered myself for the fries I thought I'd be eating.

"Thanks!" I dipped a couple of the fries in and ate them as I watched Nolan wind up again. That time I was ready for the loud slap and loved the expression of triumph on Nolan's face when the batter stepped out of the box as the umpire called a strike. I saw Nolan hold his shoulder for a second and rotate his arm. I worried that he'd hurt it again.

When Nolan turned his attention back to home plate, I could see a small grimace. When he looked up into the stands again, he shook his head ever so slightly, letting me know it wasn't too bad. The anxiety in my gut let up a little and I exhaled a sigh of relief. I watched the rest of his pitches closely, looking for any sign that he was hurting.

When the inning switched from the top to the bottom, he jogged into the dugout and headed for his bag. I stood and made my way past his brothers to the small snack bar and grabbed an ice pack. By the time I reached the dip in the gate near the old wooden dugout, he was already making his way to me. I handed him the ice pack and he gave me my kit.

"Thanks," we both said, and then laughed.

"Do you think you hurt it again?" I asked, concerned.

"I don't know. It feels really tight." He rotated his shoulder and I reached out and rubbed it with my hand.

"If you can't handle it, I'm ready," Henry called from the dugout. Nolan's jaw tightened, but I held on to his shoulder so he wouldn't make a move he'd regret.

"Doctor said you should take it easy this year. How many innings does the coach have you pitching?" I asked.

"Three for right now. I'm fourth to bat and we're going to

see how I feel after. He wants to keep my count low so he can save me for playoffs. I should go," he said, looking over his shoulder at the batter finishing warming up.

I stood at the fence a little longer, watching him duck back inside. I took a minute to check my blood sugar and then I headed back up to the bleachers. Erin's head was buried in her phone, but as I made my way to our seats, she looked up at me and asked, "Did he hurt his shoulder?"

"It's an old injury. He's not sure if he reinjured it or if it's just tight." I put my kit down between us and reached for the drink on the bench near both his brothers.

"Regular," Seth said. Gavin handed me his drink instead and I took a long sip of the diet soda to wash down the fries. When I reached for more, the bag was empty. Seth shrugged.

Our moms were just as ridiculous when Nolan came up to bat. I tried hard not to laugh when shouts of "Show 'em how it's done, number seven!" and "Home run, Nolan!" flew like a flurry of snowflakes in a blizzard behind me. Erin looked up long enough to watch him rip one out to far right field. We cheered loudly as he passed first base and headed for second. The outfielder tried to get the ball in quickly, but he didn't quite make it and Nolan stopped safely on the base.

The rest of the game seemed to fly by as I watched Nolan and talked with his brothers about school. Our team won the game seven to five, and we moved from the bleachers to the fence and waited for the boys to pack up their gear. Nolan's parents gave me hugs good-bye and told Erin they were looking forward to seeing her again soon.

When Nolan finally emerged from the dugout, the ice pack on his shoulder was filthy with red clay and grass. It didn't seem to matter, though, and that's when I knew he was hurting worse than he was letting on. I wanted to reach for him again, but felt like it would be disrespectful to do that in front of Erin. Instead I just fell in step behind them as we made our way out to his truck.

"Thanks for inviting me," Erin said when we pulled up in front of her house. "It was a lot of fun."

"Thanks for coming." Nolan leaned over and gave her a quick kiss. "I'd walk you to the door but I really need to get home and put some more ice on this quick." She looked a tad bit hurt but seemed to shake it off.

"See you tomorrow," she said as she stepped down out of the truck. We waited outside until he was sure she'd gotten in safely. He pulled away from the curb and drove down a few house lengths until we were out of sight.

Pulling over again, he asked, "Can you drive? This shoulder's fucking killing me." I'd like to think he was hiding the severity of his pain from Erin because he wanted my help instead of hers, but Nolan had a lot of pride so maybe he just didn't know her well enough yet to let her see him in a moment of weakness. He put the truck in park and scooted over to the passenger side. Being the lady I was, I climbed over the seat, banging my head and managing to tumble a bit before righting myself behind the wheel. He looked at me with an amused expression. "We don't need both of us hurt, Zie."

"Zip it." I put the truck in drive and got us home safely. It was just getting dark by the time we pulled into his driveway. I had some homework I needed to finish up, but I wasn't really in the mood to start it.

Nolan used his good arm to open the tailgate, but I reached up and grabbed his bag so he wouldn't have to carry it in. "I can carry my own bag," he said.

"I'm not taking any chances. You were such a whiner." I was teasing, of course. He'd actually been very strong during his recovery. He worked extra hard with the physical therapist to make sure he'd be cleared to play this year. That was all the more reason my heart was hurting for the setback he was experiencing.

When we got to his room, I put his bag down near his closet. "Are you going to shower up and get some rest?" I asked as he struggled to pull his jersey off. Without much thought, I grabbed its hem and pulled it up and off his body. He winced again at the angle his shoulder had to make to get the jersey over his head.

"Actually I think I'm going to sit in the hot tub for a while. The ice didn't help, so I'm hoping the heat will loosen it up. Feel like sitting with me?" His hands moved to his belt and he unbuckled it and pulled it through the loops. He toed off his cleats and reached down to pull his socks off but couldn't manage it with his shoulder hurting.

"I can sit with you for a little while." I put my hand flat against his warm chest and pushed him playfully back so he tumbled onto his bed. Dropping down, I pulled off his socks one at a time. When I straightened back up, he was staring at me, propped up on his good arm and leaning to the side. The sight of him made my cheeks flush and I felt a small earthquake inside my stomach. He was just so breathtaking. The picture before me could have been an ad for men's underwear.

We didn't say a word to each other. When I took a tiny step back in an attempt to break the spell, he sat up and reached for my arm. His strong fingers wrapped around my wrist and he pulled me a little closer. I waited for him to say something, but he just looked up at me like he couldn't put the words together. The sound of the front door opening brought us back down to reality and he quickly released my arm and looked away.

"Go get your suit," he said as I backed up and he stood.

I didn't look back as I took a few steps on my way out of

his room. When I turned the knob and opened the door, his voice seemed to float over my shoulder and down into my soul. "Thanks, Zie."

"Of course." I pulled his door shut behind me and headed downstairs.

"How's he doing?" his mom asked as she set her purse down on the counter.

"It's really sore. I think it's hurting more than he's admitting." His mom nodded and I could see the worry in her eyes. So much of Nolan's future was riding on his scholarship for baseball. If he couldn't finish the season, there was a chance he would lose it. I wasn't sure what would happen if he didn't get the scholarship because we never talked about that. It felt like talking about that possibility gave it power somehow, and no one wanted to put that negative energy out there. Nolan's dad put his hands on Mrs. Walker's shoulders, and I got the impression that even though Nolan and I hadn't discussed the possibility that he might lose the scholarship, they certainly had.

"He's going to be fine," his dad reassured us. I nodded and smiled, hoping against all odds that he was right.

fourteen

MY FEET WERE cold as I made my way across the wet grass and up to the gate. I should have worn my flip-flops, but my thoughts had been focused on hurrying back to Nolan. I opened the latch and slipped into his yard. The sound of the hot tub bubbling echoed through the otherwise quiet night.

"Set up the Bluetooth on your phone to the speakers. You can pick the playlist," he said from the edge of the hot tub. His legs were in the water from just below his knees down, and he was massaging his injured shoulder mindlessly as he watched the bubbles formed by the jets chasing each other around.

I quickly set up the music and chose my country playlist. I set my phone and kit down on the lounge chair next to the one that had Nolan's towel and flip-flops. It was still a little chilly outside so I tried to hurry so I wouldn't get too cold in my bikini. Unclipping my pump, I slipped the small disconnect cover into the cannula housing and then wrapped the tubing around my pump and set it down on top of my towel.

I sat on the edge of the hot tub and kicked my feet in the swirling water. "How's it feeling?" I asked.

"Not sure yet. I didn't feel anything snap or pop, but there was this sharp pain when I released the ball. Now it just aches. Maybe I didn't warm up enough."

"That sucks." I kicked at the water and leaned back on my hands. I was glad I'd remembered to pull my hair up into a messy bun on the top of my head. The smell of chlorine seemed to take forever to wash out. The music was interrupted for a second and then resumed playing, which meant I had received a text message. My parents knew where I was and chances were, it was just the group text I was included on where Nisha and Regan were discussing *The Bachelor* spoilers they had accidentally seen online. I was just about to submerge more of my body into the water when it happened again.

"You should get that or it's going to drive me crazy." Nolan bumped my shoulder with his good one. I twisted around and set my feet back on the steps. I could feel his eyes on me as I made my way over to my phone.

JUDE: Hey Mackenzie.

JUDE: Is Italian ok for Friday?

My lips curled up as I typed back a response.

ME: I love Italian.

JUDE: Then it's settled. Can't wait to see you again.

"Who's making you smile?" Nolan asked when I set my phone down and headed back toward him.

"It was Jude asking about dinner Friday." I climbed up the steps and decided to just go for it and sit down on the seat beneath the water. My back stung for a second but quickly adjusted. Nolan slipped off the edge and into the water too. He let out a hiss when his shoulders dipped below the scorching surface.

"Are you getting excited about your date?" He moved his good hand across the surface of the water, gathering the bubbles and then letting them go.

"Excited and nervous, I guess." I closed my eyes and slipped lower so my neck was submerged as well.

"What are you nervous about? Just be yourself."

"I don't even know what I'm supposed to do, Nolan. Do we hold hands? Do I offer to pay for dinner?" I sighed and opened my eyes, looking at him. The jets tossed me around a little and our bodies had moved apart to slip comfortably into the seats in each corner.

"He'll pay for dinner because he asked you. Hold his hand if it feels right." He put his good arm up across the back of the hot tub. I'd never even held a boy's hand besides Nolan's. I wasn't sure any other hand would ever feel right in mine.

"Do you think he'll be able to tell that I've never kissed anyone before?" I sat up and folded my arms on the edge so I could rest my head.

Nolan thought for a minute. I could tell the question had caught him off guard. "I guess that will depend on how good you are at doing it." He looked away for a second. "Even if he figures it out, I don't think that would make him not like you. I think it would be kind of cool to be someone's first kiss." His hand dipped back into the water and he rubbed at his hurt shoulder.

"Come here," I said, waving him over to me. He hesitated for a minute but then slid along the seat until he was in front of me. I opened and closed my hands to show him that I wanted to massage his shoulder. He grinned and turned around so he could sit between my legs. "Tell me if I hurt you."

My fingers gently traced his skin, from his neck to his shoulder and back. When he didn't flinch or move away, I made the same movement again with more pressure. "That feels really good," he said, relaxing back into me. My skin was touching his, and the places where we were connected were suddenly even hotter than they had been from the water. I made the trail with my hands back out to his shoulder.

"Any pointers you could give me, Mr. Experienced?" I teased. He'd told me tons of stories over the years of his adventures with girls, but I couldn't recall anything specific that would make me feel more prepared for what was happening on Friday. I already had plans to call Nisha and Regan later to talk more about it. We'd been discussing it all week and I knew they'd be excited to hear a guy's perspective.

"You're really nervous, aren't you?" he asked with disbelief. His hands rested on my knees beneath the surface. He leaned his head to the side so I could have better access to the muscles in his neck. "I don't think there's anything you could do to screw it up, Zie. You're overthinking everything. Just relax and enjoy yourself. Don't let him push you further than you want to go. That's pretty much all I can give you." He turned his head so he could see my face.

"Okay. I'll just relax and see what happens." It was a lie. I was going to stress out about Friday for the rest of the week.

Nolan was easygoing. Everyone loved him and he always knew the right things to say and do. I couldn't get past imagining this horrible disaster of a kiss or getting food stuck in my teeth during dinner.

"You're not relaxing," he said, and I realized I'd been staring off into space as I rubbed his tight shoulder muscles. I shook my head and blew out a big breath. He turned his body so that he was almost entirely facing me. His thigh brushed up against mine on the seat and I almost squeezed my legs around it. He laughed and grabbed my wrists. "Quit freaking out about it."

"Easy for you to say!" I tried to slip free from his grip but he just grinned at me and brought my hands beneath the water. "This is all new to me. I don't like feeling like I'm going to mess something up."

"It doesn't have to be perfect, Sugar. It's just a first date. Maybe you will be nervous. Maybe you'll struggle to find something to say to each other over dinner. Maybe he'll even hold your hand the wrong way." We both laughed because we knew the right way to hold hands was to lace your fingers together; it was something we'd discussed and agreed on in fourth grade. I moved my eyes back up to his. "And maybe you'll need a little more practice kissing. None of it will matter if he gets to know you."

"If you say so," I said, and he released my wrists. He

watched my face, searching for a sign that I truly agreed with him and wouldn't worry anymore. When he tipped his head to the side as if to say *really?* all I could do was shrug. He let out a strangled laugh and rubbed his hand over his face.

"You're infuriating sometimes," he said as he stared straight into my eyes. "You get so deep into this head of yours, you sabotage yourself." He tapped my head a few times lightly with his finger. "I can't believe you're really that worried about it." When I didn't say anything, I knew he could read all of my self-doubt in my face. I didn't move and neither did he. Finally, he righted his head and whispered, "Do you trust me?"

"Yes," I whispered back without any hesitation. His hand emerged from the water and moved to the side of my face. He leaned in close to me and I watched his eyes until he was so close I could feel his skin brush against mine. His lips touched my lips softly as his hand tilted my head up just slightly and his thumb brushed across my cheek.

I couldn't believe it was happening. Nolan Walker was kissing me. Every other thought in my mind got quiet as his lips parted and his tongue slipped between my own parted lips. I hadn't even realized I was opening my mouth for him, but there he was, his tongue caressing my own as our lips met again and again. I grew dizzy from the sensation of it and steadied myself with my hands on the outsides of his shoulders. My chest pressed up against him as I arched toward his body, needing to get closer and closer.

Breathless, he pulled away, and I tried hard to open my eyes, which were heavy with lust and euphoria. His hand slowly left my face and I felt my chest rising and falling with the deep breaths I was pulling in. My heart was pounding so quickly that I could almost hear my pulse in my ears. I thought that I should say something, but wasn't sure what that something was. I waited, hoping he didn't regret what had just happened.

I watched so many emotions pass behind his eyes. Inside I was hoping that kiss had meant as much to him as it had meant to me. Maybe it hadn't been his intention, but I couldn't imagine he hadn't felt it the way I had.

Finally he spoke, his voice thick and tight. "Now you don't have to worry so much about your first kiss." The words were a whisper between us. I felt the emotion rise up in my throat and worried it would all spill out in a mess of admissions I wasn't ready to give him yet. He was waiting for me to say something, and I couldn't get past how happy and hopeful I'd been a few minutes ago and how devastated I felt as I looked at him and realized that he wasn't about to make some grand declaration of love for me.

"Thanks" was all I could manage. I thought for a second he looked disappointed too, but his face quickly changed and he moved away from me and out of the hot tub. I followed him out in silence and wrapped my towel around me. It felt awful and painful and oh so confusing. I grabbed my pump and kit and Nolan grabbed his towel and slipped his finger beneath the straps of his flip-flops. The music fell silent as I shut down my playlist. "I'll see you tomorrow," I managed to say, pushing past the tightness in my chest and throat. He didn't answer; he just stood there watching me leave.

I felt the first tear when I reached the gate and hurried to open the latch. "Zie?" he called to me. I didn't turn around but I stopped fiddling with the stupid gate latch. He took my pause as a sign to continue. "I was wrong." The sharpest pain shot through my heart at that exact moment, and I worried I would crumble right there in his yard. Just as I found the strength to unlatch the fence, he said, "You don't need any more practice kissing."

The latch sprang open and I practically fell into my yard. When I turned around, he was gone.

fifteen

THURSDAY MORNING I felt rattled all the way to my bones as I got ready for the day. I couldn't think about what had happened because every time I remembered any moment from last night, my stomach twisted and my heart raced as if it was happening all over again. Why did I have to crush so hard on my best friend? I felt silly for even letting myself believe in that short moment that he might have shared some of the same feelings I had. That kiss last night might have been my first, but it was just one of many for Nolan.

Last night as I lay awake in my bed, all I could think

about was how hurt I was that our kiss hadn't mattered to Nolan. I wasn't sure if I was supposed to pretend it didn't matter to me or if I even could. By morning, though, I had come to the conclusion that I had no other choice if I wanted to keep Nolan as a friend.

I finished straightening my hair and unplugged the flatiron. I might have even given myself a little pep talk in the mirror about acting normal when I went over to Nolan's house before school. Before I left my room, I pulled out the small drawer in my desk and found one of the lists we'd written together when we were younger—REASONS WE ARE THE BEST, BEST FRIENDS—and tucked it into my back pocket to remind myself my heartbreak would pass, but my friendship with him would always be there.

His mother was sitting at the table in their kitchen drinking coffee. I set my bag down near the table. "Good morning."

"Good morning," she answered. "I heard him up there banging around so I think he might have actually gotten up on time today." She first blew a tiny puff of air onto the steaming coffee and then took a small sip.

"How's his shoulder?"

"You'll have to ask him. We were in bed before he came in last night. I'm still hoping he just wasn't warmed up enough. I'm sick thinking he might have to go through all that again."

She shook her head and set her coffee down. "I'm trying not to hover, but it's taking all the strength I have." She smiled tightly at me and reached for the newspaper.

"You know you can read that on your phone now, right? No more black fingers?" I took a few steps toward the stairs.

"There's just something about holding the real thing that makes it better." She opened the paper and began to read the small black print. I made my way up the stairs and paused outside his room. The door was cracked open, but I didn't feel like I could just push my way through like I had in the past. I hated that.

I closed my eyes and steadied my heart rate, then decided I wasn't going to let anything change what we had. I pushed open his door and was met with the humid heat of a morning shower. "Is that you, Zie?" he yelled from inside the bathroom.

"Yes," I answered loudly over the sound of the running water.

"I'll be out in a minute." I nodded even though he couldn't see me. I moved to rest against his desk, but a new set of nearly naked models on his board caught my attention. It made me smile, and of course I went to work on their winter outfits. I leaned back on the edge of the old wooden desk as I cut each girl a full parka, scarf, and rain boots. I heard the shower water shut off and hurried to finish gluing the new outfits on their owners. There weren't many scraps left to push into his trash can, but you can't blame me because if it weren't for me, those poor young ladies would have frozen in those tiny bikinis.

"Um, a little help in here?" he called from the bathroom. I pushed open the door and found him with the towel wrapped around his waist. He had sweat across his brow and a scowl on his face. I noticed the boxer briefs on the floor and the way they were tangled around his foot. His hand was squeezing his bad shoulder protectively and I knew he was in a world of pain just by the tight, hard features that were now softening into a look of defeat.

"Are you okay?"

"I can't do anything that requires any resistance with my fucking shoulder," he answered. "Can you," he started, and then shook his head. His eyes dropped down to the floor to where his boxers were. "Can you please help me get dressed?"

"Sure. How should I, um, what should . . ." I was stumbling all over my words, not quite sure how I would be able to help him.

"I'll move my feet. I just can't pull them up with one arm." He dropped his good arm down and gripped his towel where it was tucked at his waist. I squatted down and opened the waist on the boxers as big as I could. He stepped into them, kicking a little to get his foot through the leg hole. I tugged them up, stopping at the bottom of the towel.

"What are you going to do? Maybe it's time to go back to the doctor?" I looked up into the reflection of his eyes in the mirror in front of us.

"I'm going to call him today." He sighed. "I'll hang on to my towel if you can pull them up underneath it."

I held on to the waist of the boxers on each side and stood up fully, moving them up beneath his damp towel. It took a little maneuvering to get them all the way up, so I kept my eyes turned toward the shower in case the towel curtain failed. He used his good arm to make a few adjustments. When everything was where he wanted it, he pulled the towel from around his waist and stood before me in just his boxers. I tried to look everywhere except where I shouldn't.

Next, I grabbed his shorts and held them open for him to step into. I kept my face turned away from his as I shimmied them up his legs. When they were finally around his waist, he tried to button them. His eyes closed as he fumbled with the button, and finally he sighed loudly and reached for his bad shoulder. "It hurts to make even little movements. Dammit." He tipped his head back and opened his eyes, staring at the ceiling as if to ask the heavens why this was happening to him.

"It's fine," I assured him. "I can do it." I stepped in front of him and took the top of his shorts into my hands, pulling them together to fasten the button. His head tipped forward again and I could feel him watching my movements. I looked up into his eyes and gave him a small, reassuring smile. "It's going to be okay." My fingers pinched the zipper and I dragged it up to the button. Without waiting for him to direct me, I grabbed his shirt off the sink and rolled the hem up and opened the neck wide.

"Thank you," he said softly. I pulled the shirt over his head and down to his shoulders. He easily got his good arm through and then took in a deep breath in anticipation of when we'd have to put his hurt shoulder to work. I pulled it over as far as I could so he didn't have to manipulate the joint much. I hated seeing the pain on his face as he finally managed to get his arm into the hole. Quickly, I rolled the T-shirt down the rest of the way and then put my hands on my hips and gave him a big grin.

"That wasn't so bad," I teased. I smoothed his shirt over his chest.

"Think I can shave with my left hand?" he asked, turning his head to see his scruff in the mirror. "It gets itchy if I don't keep it shaved." He pulled open a drawer and retrieved his shaving cream and razor. I shrugged.

"I'll do it. It can't be that different from shaving my legs." With a little reluctance, he handed me the razor. I set it on the counter and shook up the shaving cream. The foam expanded on the palm of my hand just before I rubbed my palms together and then spread the tiny bubbles over his cheeks and chin. He laughed when I wiped the rest of the cream onto his nose.

The first few strokes of the razor across his skin were nerve-racking. I worried I was pushing down too hard or that I'd cut him as I moved the blades over his jaw. When I didn't nick him, though, my bravery grew and I slid the razor with ease. He reached behind me and turned on the hot water so I could rinse it. I used the counter as leverage to raise myself up and sit on it. Even with my attention zoned in on his freshly shaven skin, I could feel his eyes on me. I'd be nervous too if he had a sharp object near me.

I looked into his eyes, and the same thought that had visited my consciousness over the last few years floated in again. *I love you.* There had been a few times where the thought alone was so powerful it almost left my lips. I knew better then, just like I knew not to let it escape in that moment. Those three words would change things, and even if there was never a doubt in my mind that we could be so wonderful together, I had no idea what was going through his head and heart. His eyes met mine and we seemed to freeze for a minute.

"We're going to be late," he said. "I'm sorry."

"Don't be. It doesn't really matter." I dragged the razor down his cheek one last time and then ran it through the water. I shut it off and set the razor on the counter.

"I'll wait out there for you," I said, motioning to his bedroom. "Just call for me if you need anything else." His eyes dipped down for just a second and then he nodded.

I sat on the edge of his unmade bed and waited for him to finish up. When he emerged from the bathroom, he headed to his closet and grabbed a pair of shoes. He could probably put them on without much movement to his shoulder, but why take a chance that he'd aggravate the injury any further? I stood and moved to his dresser, opening his sock drawer and finding a pair. He took my place at the edge of his bed.

"I can do it," he said. "Just help me get my socks on."

"Don't be silly. You help me all the time. I can tie your shoes once in a while." I unfolded the socks and pulled them onto his feet. I put one shoe in front of his foot and he slipped it inside. I did the same with the other. My fingers found the ends of the laces and as I began to tie them my hair fell in front of me. His fingers casually tucked it behind my ears from above.

"Let's not go to school today." His words stopped my fingers and I looked up at him. "I can't carry my bag or use my good hand. Let's go to breakfast and maybe catch a movie.

I've got to call the doctor and get an appointment, but it probably won't be until later this afternoon."

We'd done it a handful of times already over the years on days my numbers were off. When I was younger, the school had to keep a nurse on staff to administer insulin. In the state of California, the rules were such that only a trained nurse could do the job. Whenever the nurse was sick or took the day off, I'd usually just stay home so it wouldn't be a big hassle trying to get someone there to take care of me or have my mother running back and forth to the school to approve the dose. On those days, Nolan would stay home with me too.

As we grew up, we continued the tradition by taking a few days off here and there to spend them together. We'd hang out, rent movies, and order a pizza, or if we were lucky one of our parents would take us somewhere fun. Now that we were older and could drive ourselves, we'd sometimes stay home and find ways to entertain ourselves, usually by grabbing something to eat and then binge-watching a series on Netflix.

"Sounds a lot better than school." I stood up and took a few steps back. His smile was warm and grateful. "Were you thinking Spires or the Pancake House?"

"Spires," he answered with a wide grin. There was something about the pale pink booths and the worn green flowery carpet that had always served as a pick-me-up when things weren't going our way. We'd eaten there after he got his appendix out two years ago and again when he had his shoulder surgery. I'd also needed the homey comfort the morning after Roxie, my Chihuahua, had passed away, and when I didn't make president of our class freshman year.

He grabbed his baseball cap off the dresser and left his backpack next to his desk. I followed him down the stairs and into the kitchen, where his mom was still sitting at the table. "Mom, can we ditch today? We want to go to Spires for breakfast and then maybe we'll catch a movie if we have time before I can get in with the doc." Nolan grabbed his keys off the counter and tossed them to me.

"If you're sure it's okay with your mom," she answered, looking at me.

"I'll ask," I promised.

"Okay. Have a good time. Let me know when the appointment is when you find out." She gave us a small wave and then returned her attention back to the newspaper. A lot of my friends had to sneak around when they didn't want to go to school. Nolan and I were lucky our parents didn't seem to mind a day off here and there as long as it wasn't abused and we made up all the work.

On the way to his truck, I shot my mom a quick text asking her if she was okay with our change of plans. She replied that it was okay and to be careful. I opened Nolan's door for him and he gave me a look that said he wasn't completely amused with my mothering. Once in the driver's seat, I tucked my phone away and fired up the engine. The truck was his prized possession and I was pretty sure that the only people besides him who had ever driven it were his dad and me. It was a small club I was very honored to be a part of.

sixteen

NOLAN HELD THE old glass door open with his good arm as an elderly couple made their way into Spires before us. We waited for one of the waitresses to motion for us to seat ourselves and then slid into our usual booth in our favorite waitress's section. She let us know she saw us as she hurried past with a hot pot of coffee.

A group of older gentlemen were sitting at a large table made from a few smaller ones all pushed together. There were also four middle-aged men sitting together in a booth across from us. Their Bibles were out and they were discussing passages as they waited for their breakfast. Nolan had chosen correctly. I knew from experience that it was going to be an interesting day to eat there.

Our waitress flew by our table, dropping off my diet soda and Nolan's coffee. We didn't have to tell her our drink orders since we'd come there enough that she knew what we'd want. As I tapped the straw on the table to remove it from its wrapper, the large group of men began to sing. They were a well-practiced men's choir, and although it wasn't anything like the music we normally listened to, it would've been hard not to enjoy the nostalgic fifties sound. I glanced around and loved seeing the older patrons snapping along or swaying with their music.

When the song ended, the entire restaurant broke out in applause. The waitresses had continued to scurry around as if a group of men singing in the middle of a restaurant wasn't anything unusual. Our waitress stopped at our table again to check that we wanted our usual order. We barely had time to agree before she was off to help another table. That's why she was our favorite.

It was just past nine when Nolan pulled out his phone and called the doctor's office. I listened as he made himself a three o'clock appointment. When he finished the call, he set his phone on the table near the napkin dispenser. Instantly the screen lit up with an incoming call. He pressed the button on the side to silence the ringing, but didn't answer it or send it immediately to voice mail.

"You can answer it," I said, putting the straw to my lips for a sip of my soda. I saw that it was Erin, and I didn't want our breakfast together to cause any trouble between them. I felt guilty suddenly for what had happened last night.

"Nah, it's okay." The screen went dim again. The silence that followed felt miserably awkward. Nolan bent the brim of his cap as if he needed something to do with his hands. He blew out a breath. "Do you think I should tell her?"

The guilt I felt grew, and I could see how torn up Nolan was about that decision. Even though they weren't exclusive and clearly the kiss meant nothing to him, it might mean something to her if she found out about it. It could ruin their relationship.

"I don't know. I won't tell anyone. She won't ever hear about it from me." I played with my drink as I watched him think about his options.

"We haven't said we wouldn't be with other people, but you're not just some other person. It took a while to convince her that you and I were just friends, and I think if I were honest with her she wouldn't trust me anymore. She wouldn't believe that it was innocent." He folded his arms tightly across his chest.

Last night it had hurt to see him unaffected by our kiss, but at least I hadn't seen regret. Sitting in that booth, I got a front row seat to watch him think about how he wished he hadn't kissed me. It magnified the pain I had been feeling until it nearly choked me.

"It didn't mean anything," I lied. "You were just helping a friend. It was impulsive and a mistake. It's not going to happen again so maybe you shouldn't mention it."

His eyes stayed locked on mine, as if he was looking for something in them. "So it isn't worth mentioning?" he asked.

I shook my head. "It's only going to hurt her. Let's just forget it ever happened."

"That's what you want?" Nolan asked, and I was beginning to feel like I was gaining some control again. I couldn't go back and stop it from happening, but I could write the narrative on the role it played in our friendship, and right now I was writing it in as a tiny footnote instead of giving it its own chapter.

I nodded.

"Okay." He opened a small creamer and poured its contents into his steaming hot coffee. He reached for another creamer. "I'm really sorry, Zie. I know I've put you in a position where you're going to have to keep a secret too. I should never have kissed you." The cream formed a tan cloud in his coffee before he stirred it in.

"You were trying to help me. It was my fault too." I swirled my soda with the straw.

We fell silent as our waitress approached our table with our breakfasts. She set the plates down and slid a bottle of Tabasco sauce toward Nolan before he'd even had a chance to ask for it.

"Thank you, Zie," Nolan said when we were alone again.

I smiled at him even though I was sure a little part of my heart was cracking. It was settled. He wasn't going to tell Erin about our mistake and I was going to keep our secret.

I unzipped my purse and opened my kit. Nolan watched me as he aimlessly moved his eggs around his plate. I quickly tested myself, administering the insulin for the food I was about to eat, and then I tucked my kit away again. Nolan scooped up some eggs, concentrating hard on not spilling them using his left hand as I took the first bite of my bacon. "I'm going to miss this place when we're away at college."

I laughed around my mouthful of breakfast. "Me too. There are a lot of things I'm going to miss," I said, smiling at him so it was clear I was talking about him. The only comfort I could give myself was to think about how determined we both were to remain friends. Even if it wouldn't always be exactly how I wanted it, we'd still have each other in our lives. "You always had great ideas about what kind of trouble we could get into to keep busy."

"I'm full of great ideas," Nolan said. "And maybe a bad one or two," he added as an afterthought as he nudged my foot beneath the table. I knew it was his way of continuing to take the blame for the kiss last night. I gave him a lopsided smile to let him know I accepted his joke and was cool with moving on from last night.

We both ate our breakfasts without talking until Nolan looked up from his plate and glanced around. "Why is it so quiet in here?" he asked. "I feel like there should be some background tunes or something."

Apparently Nolan had magical powers, because as soon as the words were out of his mouth, the men's choir began to sing. We both fought our laughter, but lost in the end.

"What kind of sorcery was that?" I asked through my laugh.

"Don't question my powers," he commanded in a booming voice, quickly scrunching his napkin into a ball and tossing it at me. Sometimes I wondered if being friends since we were young had stunted the maturity of our behavior while in public together. Sure, we'd just had a good heart-to-heart, but in the end it always boiled down to playing around like a couple of ten-year-olds.

We clapped when the song ended and went back to our breakfasts with grins still on our faces. From across the table he asked, "Do you have a pen?" I gave him a curious look but dug around in my kit until I found one.

"Sure. What do you need it for?" I held it over the center

of the table and only realized when he didn't reach for it that I'd have to be the one to do the writing.

"I think we should make a list," Nolan said.

"That's a great idea." I couldn't wait to create another list with him. I could still feel the one I had tucked into my pocket that I'd brought with me and I couldn't think of a better way to get our friendship back on track.

"Let's make a list of all the things we have loved doing together over the years. We're going to revisit every single one of them before summer. It will be a celebration of our friendship—kind of like a huge graduation party as we move from childhood friends to adult friends. It will be our 'Senior Year Bucket List.'"

"This sounds like the best idea!" A thought occurred to me. "I thought these types of lists were for things you've never done that you want to do before you die." My bad habit of chewing on the ends of pens took over and I found myself clenching the cap between my front teeth.

"We're going to do that too. Let's put down everything we've loved and everything we can think of that we want to experience together but haven't had the chance to yet. We'll change the title to 'Senior Year Redo Bucket List.'"

"I like that. You go first."

"Do you remember when we camped out in my yard when we graduated fifth grade? I want to do that again." I remembered that night very well. I woke up with two mosquito bites on my forehead.

"Okay, but you're bringing the bug spray." I grabbed a clean napkin from the stack at the end of the table and wrote *camp out* on the list.

"Deal. Your turn."

"Fine. Do you remember when Patrick Bower made fun of you for that terrible haircut you got? We snuck out at night and met up." I waited for the recognition to set in.

"How many rolls of toilet paper did we use? That was ridiculous but totally vindicating. Write it down. It's time to revisit that for sure. We'll worry about who our target is later."

I wrote down *late night TP party.* "I believe it was sixteen rolls."

"Go big or go home, huh?"

"Thank God your mom has a Costco card. Nothing beats buying the toilet paper in bulk. I can't believe our moms agreed it was a good idea." Nolan's mother had been furious at Patrick for teasing Nolan in front of his friends. If he had lived farther away than the one block, I'm pretty sure she would have signed up to be our getaway driver.

"My turn. There are so many things I'd want to do again but we'd never finish this list before summer. I'm trying to pick out just the highlights. Let's see—I want to go to Disneyland again. Just you and me so we can ride Space Mountain a million times if we want." Last time we'd gone there we had to go on all the rides his brothers and our parents wanted to go on too. I agreed and wrote *Disneyland* on our list.

"Oh, we are definitely running through the park sprinklers at night. That was awesome!"

"That's a good one," he chuckled. I wrote *epic sprinklers* and immediately wondered if they would feel as epic now that we were older. It didn't matter; I had to do it at least one more time with him.

"If we think of anything else that has to be on that list, we can add it. Let's come up with a few things we've never done. I'll go first; I want to get a tattoo," he said.

"Like you want me to go with you while you get it?" I asked.

"No, like I want us to get tattoos together. They don't have to be huge and something terrible we'll always regret, but just something small to say we got our first tattoos together. You can even pick what we get." He took a sip of his coffee and then set it down and pushed the napkin a little closer to me so I'd write it down.

I lifted an eyebrow in question, but I could see by the seriousness in his expression he wasn't joking. "What if I pick something ridiculous? That's too much pressure."

"If you can't think of something to get, I'll pick. Let's just see what happens when we get there." He looked back down at his plate and began spearing the breakfast potatoes with his fork. I wrote down *tattoos* and instantly felt excitement as the idea washed over me. Somehow committing to it on a napkin made it more real and I started falling in love with the idea.

"I don't think any friendship can be complete without a road trip. If we can't manage that, then all of this will be for nothing," I teased dramatically. "Maybe we can go for a day or two over spring break. It doesn't have to be anywhere too far, just enough to be disconnected from everyone and experience life on the road." *Road trip* made our list without any argument. He simply nodded and gave me a playful smile. In that moment I might have been the happiest I'd ever been.

"Eat your breakfast." He pointed his fork at my plate to emphasize his command.

"Now you're just getting cocky with your left-handed fork control." We both scooped another bite of potatoes into our mouths and chewed as the men started up another tune. When breakfast was over and our waitress had dropped off the bill, I folded up our list, which felt so much more valuable than just an item used to clean a mess. I tucked it into the empty pouch of my kit since that was something that was always with me. Circumstances in our future might make it harder to be together, but we would always value and work on what we had.

seventeen

THE MOVIE THEATER was still lit up when we finally made our way to our seats. I thought it was surprising that they had been able to sell so many tickets to a movie about a billionaire and his meek love interest on a Thursday afternoon. I had clearly underestimated the amount of moviegoers who were free for an early weekday showing. Nolan followed along behind me, holding our popcorn while I moved into our favorite seats in the first row of the stadium seating so we could rest our feet on the metal bars in front of us. This movie was the only option we had besides a children's cartoon or a foreign movie with subtitles if we wanted to make it to his appointment on time.

"You are going to owe me for this!" he whisper-yelled as we sat down. I set my diet soda in the cup holder between us and exaggeratedly rolled my eyes at him.

"Don't pretend you aren't curious. Everyone is talking about this movie." I winked at the end, and it was his turn to roll his eyes.

"You can say what you want, but if I have to watch Jamie Dornan in all his full-screen glory, you are sitting through any movie I choose without question next game night."

"Oh, God, not the piranhas. Anything but that." I made a sour face as I unzipped my kit.

"Oh, there will be piranhas, or sharks, or anything that comes when lots of girls are frolicking around in the water on spring break. I can see the bikinis already." He held his hands up and framed an imaginary screen.

"I have such trouble suspending my scientific knowledge in order to believe that suddenly a man-made lake is swarming with fish found only in other countries. It's absurd." I pressed the lancet to my finger and drew a drop of blood. He chuckled while peeking over at the meter screen. When my number was normal and I'd covered myself for the snacks I was about to eat, he tilted the popcorn in my direction.

"If I have to pretend that Jamie is into Dakota, then you can pretend those vicious fish could live in a man-made lake.

Talk about suspending belief." He turned around in his seat and waved his arm across the crowded movie theater. "I want to hear from one woman here that she'd let some guy take her into that 'Red Room' if he didn't look like some Hollywood actor."

I slapped at his shoulder and laughed. "Okay, okay, okay. Stupid fish and barely legal girls in bikinis it is." My words had satisfied him, and he turned back around and slouched to get comfortable in his seat.

"Should I take notes or something?" he teased when the lights started to dim.

"You can do whatever you want, just don't get in the way of me watching the magic happen." I tossed a fallen piece of popcorn at him.

Believe it or not, he was on his best behavior throughout the entire movie. He only made a few *Yeah right* faces, but I ignored them and stayed focused on the very important and difficult plot. Okay, maybe I just watched Jamie take his shirt off.

When the lights turned back on and the theater began to empty out, he turned to me and asked, "Does that really do it for you?" I couldn't tell if he was serious so I just gave him a little push so he would continue walking out of our row. "I didn't really picture you as a paddle kind of girl." He laughed.

"Stop!" I scolded with a giggle.

"I can't even picture you in a strip club, let alone some special torture room," he said with disbelief, making an older woman smile as we passed her. I could feel my cheeks flush.

"I think I might actually crack up if someone ever danced for me. I'm too goofy for that."

"Well," he said, as if he was about to admit something big, "I think you're pretty safe with me, but if I ever do get all spun up and feel like dancing, I'll test out my moves on you. In all fairness, I'd be a little disappointed if you didn't find it funny enough to laugh." We exited the theater and made our way to his truck.

"For the sake of your ego, I hope if you ever decide to dance that way for a girl, she doesn't laugh." I moved around to the passenger side to let him in and dug for the keys in my purse.

He laughed softly. "You're right, it probably would kill my ego." It only took five minutes to drive to the doctor's office, so we decided we'd sit in the truck for the next fifteen minutes before his appointment. I found a nice spot under a big tree where we could hang out. I killed the engine but left the music playing.

"So when should we start our list?" He tapped his hand on top of my purse since my kit and the list were inside.

"What were you thinking? I'm game for whenever you want."

"Well, you have that date tomorrow, and I promised Erin I'd take her out too. How about we start with our campout Saturday night?"

"Sure. I'll bring the chips and salsa, you bring the bug spray."

"Do you still have a sleeping bag that fits you? I don't think I've ever seen you use one besides that *Beauty and the Beast* thing you had last time."

I laughed at the memory of that monstrosity. I'd insisted on sleeping in it as a child so often that it didn't properly zip anymore and my feet had wiggled a big hole at the seams. "I'll get a new one later. Should I grab a tent too?"

He didn't answer right away. He seemed to be weighing some decision. Finally he said, "I was thinking it might be kind of cool to sleep under the stars. What do you think?"

"I think that's very cliché of you," I answered, "but I also think it sounds great." He nodded his head with a grin.

"That's if I don't have to get pushed into surgery or something today." He looked up at the windows of the tall building.

"I hope that isn't the case." We sat there in silence for a while longer. We both knew that another surgery would take him out for the rest of the season. It was unclear what exactly that would do to his USC offer, but to Nolan, sitting the bench would be tragic. He truly loved the game and had loved it since the first time he stood on that T-ball field when he was five. I couldn't tell you how many of our spring days were spent down at the Little League field when we were younger, then all over the place with his travel ball team. His heart was so far into the game that I worried what would happen if he ever had to quit playing altogether.

"You're coming up with me, right?" he asked when his appointment time approached. I never went into his doctor's appointments with him, but something told me that day that he needed me there. I nodded and turned the keys the rest of the way before removing them.

"Sure thing." We entered the building and waited for the elevator. When the doors opened a toddler came running out at full speed, his father dashing after him, trying to grab his son. His mother followed them out with a baby strapped to her chest. We stepped inside and turned to watch the family. The little boy circled around a potted plant and headed back for the elevator. He stumbled and was unable to regain balance. He tumbled to the floor and his shirt hitched up a little, revealing an insulin pump.

Nolan nudged me with his good elbow and I nodded. It always hurt my heart to see young children have to live with diabetes, but it seemed doubly unfair that he couldn't even have been two years old. When his mom met my eyes, I smiled at her and lifted the hem of my shirt to show my pump. With a little wave I said, "Stay strong," just as the elevator doors closed.

There are many challenges diabetics face, and I knew they had probably just begun to face some of them since he was so young. Sometimes the challenges I faced were small, like curious eyes on me as I tested myself in the open at a restaurant or clipped my pump to a more conspicuous place on my outfit. It could be frustrating when people gave me unsolicited, unhelpful, and incorrect advice, like that eating a healthier diet, a low-carb diet, or an organic diet would cure my disease. And it was hurtful when my peers would joke that they couldn't eat one more candy bar because they'd get diabetes. One day I hoped there would be a greater understanding of diabetes, but in the meantime all we could do was support each other and try to educate people when they were willing to learn.

The doors slid open and we stepped into the long hallway. Nolan was usually a very confident guy. He rarely got nervous, but on the few occasions he was freaking out about something big, he gave away his emotions with a few tells. First was the collar adjustment. His fingers would slip into his collar and tug as if it was choking him. Next he'd rub his hand over his head, causing wrinkles to form on his forehead.

I wished I could tell him it was going to be okay, but we both knew there was a very real possibility it wouldn't.

His feet stopped outside the door and he slowly lifted his good hand to turn the knob. I waited until he pushed the door open and then captured his hand in mine. Of course our fingers were laced together the correct way.

We hadn't even been seated for a minute when the office assistant passed a clipboard full of papers over the counter for him to fill out. He jumped up and grabbed it, but handed it to me. I filled out everything I knew about him as he watched. He struggled to sign the forms and we both held in our laughter when his signature looked like a kindergartner had written it. Then I brought the clipboard back up with his insurance card. When the assistant had finished making a copy, she gave it all back to me and told us someone would be out to get us soon.

Nolan slipped his hand back in mine as we waited. It didn't take long for a woman in scrubs to come out and call him back. I assumed I'd be staying in the waiting room, but he tugged me up from the seat and pulled me along behind him as we were given a room. The woman read through the paperwork.

"So it's your right shoulder?" she asked.

"Yes. It happened yesterday, but the doctor just did surgery last year," he answered.

"Just take off your shirt, then." She marked a few more things down in the chart. "He'll be with you in a few minutes." She left the room and shut the door behind herself.

Nolan exhaled a large breath. His left hand tangled up in the hem of his shirt, but I knew he'd need my help. I helped guide his good arm from the shirt and then slowly pulled the shirt over his head and down the hurt side. Then, as if I was channeling my mother, I folded his shirt and sat down in the chair next to the exam table.

"You do realize I'm just going to have to put that back on?" he teased.

"Zip it," I scolded him as we heard a knock on the door. The doctor entered and gave Nolan a sad look.

"What happened, Mr. Walker?" He stepped over to the sink and washed his hands as Nolan recounted the pitch that seemed to reinjure his shoulder. The doctor moved around him, twisting and rotating Nolan's bad shoulder in a way that, judging from the expression on Nolan's face, hurt like hell. By the time the doctor was finished, Nolan's brow was shiny with sweat and his face looked a tad bit green.

"What do you think?" Nolan asked almost impatiently.

"I don't think it's a full tear. You still have pretty good range of motion. Can you move it at all without help?" Nolan made a full circle with his arm, but his face pinched in agony. "I think you're just going to need to head back to physical therapy and maybe get some cortisone to help speed along the healing, but I want an MRI to be certain you didn't tear through what we fixed last year."

"How long will I be out?"

The doctor let out a slow whistle. "It's your season, isn't it?" he asked, but then continued talking without waiting for his answer. "I want you out for two weeks, and then you can go back in, but no pitching until we make sure it's healing okay on its own. What's your backup position?"

"First base," Nolan answered, but the doctor was already shaking his head.

"I think that's a bit risky, son. I'd rather see you somewhere where you got a little less action. I know baseball is your bread and butter, but if you reinjure your shoulder, it's going to be hard to convince USC to play you." He pulled out a prescription tablet and wrote down a few medications. From the drawer beneath where he was standing, he pulled out a separate pad and wrote the prescription for the MRI. He patted Nolan on the good shoulder and wished him luck. He also told him to come back in a week after the MRI and they'd start therapy and treatment then. "Take it easy until I see you next time."

With that, the doctor exited the room and left us to sit there absorbing what it all meant. Nolan looked dazed, still recovering from the exam. I reached up and took the two papers off the counter. After a few more seconds, he stood up from the table and pointed to his shirt in my lap. I tucked the papers into my purse and moved toward him. We didn't say anything as I pulled his shirt over his head and helped him guide his arms through.

We scheduled a follow-up appointment with the assistant and then headed back out to his truck. "So that wasn't so bad," I said as we sat at a red light on our way home.

"It could have been worse, I guess." He glanced at me for a minute before returning his attention to looking out the passenger window. "I won't be able to feel any relief until we get the results of the MRI. If I have to go through another surgery, it's really going to throw a wrench into my plans."

"He said he didn't think it was torn too badly. Maybe this will just be a little setback in your perfect future." I tried to be optimistic, but we both knew it wasn't my strong point. He smiled anyway, but it didn't reach his eyes. He was so worried I could feel it across the cab of the truck. A few minutes later we pulled into his driveway.

"I'm going to go in and catch up on some TV. Feel like binge-watching some reality shows with me?" Nolan slid out of his truck and I followed him. Once inside, he filled his mom in on what the doctor had said and she told him she'd get him the appointment for the MRI. I handed her the two papers from the doctor and we both made our way up to his room. He kicked off his shoes and sat down on the side of the bed, turning a little and then lying back so that he didn't have to support himself with his bad arm.

I waited until he was all settled and then positioned myself beside him. Over the years we'd had our shares of medical setbacks, usually me more than him. I guess sometimes it was easier to live with those moments when we could help each other forget them. I knew his shoulder was hurting, but I let him get distracted in the obnoxious cast and their stupid actions instead of insisting we discuss what neither of us had any control of. It was like all the times he had stayed with me when my blood sugar was rising and falling unpredictably while I fought off a cold or infection.

Sometimes I wondered what it would have been like if I'd had to do all of it alone. It would not have been the same to watch movies by myself, or even just spend the day out of school without any company. It's hard to be depressed in the company of your best friend. And even if we were back in that scary place where we had no control over how quickly he healed, together we were stronger than we ever were apart.

eighteen

NOLAN WAS A big guy. He was tall, maybe six foot two, and was built of solid muscle. He took very good care of his body and enjoyed working out to improve in his sport. So why pain medicine had such a noticeable effect on him was always a wonder. When I made it over to his house that Friday morning, his mother said, "He overslept since the prescription medication made him very sleepy. I brought him some toast with another dose about thirty minutes ago and now he's up there thudding around. He's too out of it to go to class, but he keeps insisting he has a math test his teacher said he can't make up." As if to support her story, a loud thud echoed above us.

I opened his bedroom door and found him lying on the floor next to his bed, laughing. "What the heck, Nolan? Are you okay?" I moved to sit next to him and reached to touch the back of his head to make sure he was okay. He playfully swatted my hands away.

Laughing, he sat up and rubbed at his big head. "I'm fine. I just fell back to sleep and rolled right off the edge."

"Get up. I don't think you should go to school like this, but if you are, we're going to be late and we have to get our readmits." I stood and offered him my hand to help pull him up. His pupils were constricted and his lids looked so heavy as they barely made it halfway open. At least he was awake. Last year after his surgery he couldn't even manage to keep his eyes open.

"I don't think I want to get up," he said like a mischievous toddler, but he put his hand in mine with a huge dopey smile. It was adorable.

"You're a mess, lightweight. How many pills did you take?"

He shrugged a small shrug and giggled. "My mom gave me them. Do you think she gave me too much?" His eyes narrowed slightly.

"No. Not your mother. You just never take anything. Not even an aspirin. You know you don't handle opiates too well." I tugged a little on his hand but he wasn't budging. I huffed out a big breath, unsure how I was going to get him up off the floor.

"Did you just get huffy with me, Sugar?" he asked, tugging back so that I nearly lost my balance. I laughed, reaching for his bed to steady myself.

"You deserved it. I need to get you up off the floor so we can go to school. Stop playing around." I tried to sound stern, but in reality I loved this silly Nolan.

"Quit being so serious." He smiled bigger, his eyes practically slivers. "Your cheeks are turning red." He reached up and tapped my nose with his finger, and I was a bit surprised he was able to touch it accurately and not poke me in the eye. I knew from last time that he only was sloppy for the first hour after taking the medication. "Do you know your brows get closer together with these cute little wrinkles when you're thinking about something?"

I immediately relaxed my face. It didn't fly past me, the fact that he had mentioned cute in a sentence about me. I would probably remember that uninhibited connection of words forever. "Knock it off. We have to get to school. Come on." I pulled his hand but he just laughed. I didn't give up.

"No. You come on," he countered, tugging me instead. I tumbled down and managed to catch myself before our faces smashed together, something that Nolan clearly hadn't thought about. He was flat on his back and I was still on my knees, but my body was braced over his as he bounced with laughter. I had one hand on each side of his head and one leg between his.

"Nolan!" I scolded for real that time. He bit his lip to try and hide his smile. "I could have hurt you! What if I fell on your shoulder?" I shifted slightly so that I could try to stand up.

"A, you could not hurt me. B, my shoulder is feeling a lot better." He moved it around to show me.

"It's not better, Nolan; you just can't feel it as much because of the meds. Now get up so you can eat something and drink some water. Maybe that will help." I looked down into his eyes.

"Why aren't you smiling? Come on. Lighten up. Are you really in that big of a hurry to get to school? Bor-ing!" He dragged out the last two syllables like a taunting fourth grader. It made me laugh. "That's better," he announced proudly. I tried to get up again, but he was so quick I never saw his next move coming.

I let out a small yelp as he collapsed my elbow with his hand and rolled me over so that he was on top of me. I stared up into his victorious expression. "I like it when you smile," he said as he sat up and shifted the leg that was between my own to the outside, thus effectively straddling my legs. I tried to wiggle them but he just shook his head at me.

"Nolan." I said his name warningly.

"Mackenzie," he parroted back mockingly. We both laughed. "I like it when you laugh too," he added, trapping one of my wrists in his hand and raising it above my head. "I like it when you giggle. I like it when you look all serious," he said, doing his best impression of my serious face.

"Nolan," I said again, a little more stern than the last time.

He tapped my nose with his finger and then captured my other wrist, bringing it up to join the already trapped arm. He leaned forward, and in a very low whisper he said, "I like it when you're mad too." I froze, my heart swelling in my chest. "But I like it best when those little things are all tangled up together."

I must have had a curious expression on my face, because he continued, "Do you know how I get you to do all of those things together?" He held my wrists under his hand and slowly slid his free hand down the side of my body. "I tickle you." Just like that, his hand was tickling my side. He had a look of pure joy on his face as I wiggled and giggled beneath him.

Finally I was rescued when his mom came to his room to see what all the laughing was about. "Nolan! Let her go," she laughed. "You are going to be late." Within seconds he was on his feet and using my wrists to pull me to mine.

He grabbed his bag and then mine from where I had left it near his door. "All right, all right, ladies," he chided, "I'll go. I'll go." He tossed me his keys as his mom left the room. "But you better drive."

We sat in his truck and ate bagels instead of going inside, so we were forty minutes late by the time we got our readmits from the office. I worried he might fall asleep in class, but I knew his teachers would understand if he explained his reason for being a little out of it. He was still slightly altered, but he was ten times better than he had been at his house. The day was off to an unusual start and I hoped things would get back on track before my date with Jude that evening.

I found myself daydreaming in class. I thought about what I'd wear later and how much I was looking forward to seeing Jude again. Nisha and Regan had started texting me already, asking me a million questions about how I was going to wear my hair and whether or not I'd kiss him if he made a move. My excitement was piqued and I was full of the best sort of anticipation.

By the end of second period, however, I was feeling sluggish and sleepy. My thoughts were drifting off much further, and while I was trying to pull them back so I could take notes, I found it nearly impossible. I would have to borrow Regan's lecture notes for the period because it was almost as if I wasn't even in class. I pulled my kit out of my bag and tested myself. My blood sugar was low, so I decided I'd head over to the lunch area and grab a snack from the vending machines. Regan offered to walk me, but I knew she had a question about our section test and needed to ask the teacher while she had the chance, so I waved her off.

Nolan met me after class and I motioned toward the old dark corridor that led to the antiquated machines. I felt my legs wobble a little like they were quickly turning to Jell-O. He moved his backpack to his chest and stepped in front of me, bending down so that I could climb onto his back. We weren't allowed to ride piggyback at school, but it was a rule that was sometimes overlooked for me when I was too low to walk myself.

It was rare that my blood sugar would drop low enough to make it difficult for me to walk, but on occasion it would happen. I had glucose tablets and a glucagon pen in my kit for times when my blood sugar dropped very low, but I was close enough to the vending machines that I felt safe waiting for something that wouldn't make me as nauseous. I'm not sure what had happened that caused the drop in blood sugar, but I suspected it might have been because I'd just changed my pump site earlier that morning before I went to Nolan's and maybe gave myself too much insulin for the bagel I'd eaten.

Nolan held me up the best he could with his good arm under my butt as he leaned forward so that I could enter my change into the vending machine and pick a soda. The loud bell rang above us, but we ignored it; we were going to be late no matter what we did now. Nolan reached into the slot and pulled the cold drink from the machine with his bad arm. I worried for a moment about his shoulder, but it didn't seem to be bothering him.

With drink in hand, he carried me over to the wooden bench that wrapped around an old tree in the middle of the quad. I opened the can with shaky hands and quickly took a sip, swallowing it as fast as I could. I felt dizzy and disconnected. It started to feel like I was watching a movie instead of experiencing the situation firsthand.

Nolan took the can from my hand when he saw that I was struggling with finding my mouth again. He put it to my lips slowly, making sure not to choke me when my drinking mimicked a toddler learning to drink from a cup. I could see that he was worried about me but I didn't want to assure him I was okay until I felt like I really was. The final bell rang again, letting us know we were late. The last few students from the hallways cleared out and Nolan and I were left sitting in an empty quad.

"You doing better?" he asked.

"Yes. I don't know why that happened." My words

slurred together slightly, as if my tongue was too heavy to lift.

Nolan set down the soda and used his bad arm to unzip his backpack and pull out a bottle of water. I saw that he was being more careful with his shoulder now and I worried maybe his pain meds had worn off. "Is it bugging you again?"

"A little. Not anything like yesterday. I think icing it last night helped. It still hurts, but I can move my arm without wanting to die." He took a drink from the water bottle.

We didn't move to get up yet. I needed a little longer to feel like my legs were strong enough to carry me. My eyes were still struggling to stay open. I reached for the soda can with my shaky hand and nearly missed it. It wobbled when my hand didn't capture it securely, but I managed to save it before it tipped over.

"You look drunk," Nolan said. "Aren't we a pair?" he teased.

When I finally felt like I could think straight and move without growing weak, I stood up and grabbed my bag. Nolan stood too, being a little more careful when he slipped his backpack over his hurt shoulder. "I'm glad it's feeling better," I said as I tossed the soda can into the trash and we moved together toward my third-period class.

"I have the MRI on Monday morning. I think maybe I escaped a repeat surgery."

"That would be awesome." We stopped when we were outside the classroom and I swung the door open and stepped inside. All eyes in the room seemed to snap over to us, and I gave Nolan a small wave good-bye, which he returned. The teacher looked up too, giving Nolan a small nod and a little wave as the door shut and closed him out. I took my seat next to Nisha.

"Everything okay?" she whispered as soon as everyone had turned their attention back to the teacher and her lecture.

"I was low."

Nisha nodded. "Test next week." She pointed to the far right corner of the board where the announcement was printed.

"Thanks," I told her as I unzipped my bag and retrieved my notebook.

Her eyes watched as I flipped through the pages to find a blank sheet to write notes on. When Nolan's handwriting caught her eye, she reached across the aisle and stopped me by placing her hand on our list titled TOP TEN MOVIES WE'LL NEVER ADMIT TO WATCHING. I tried to flip the page, but Nisha held her hand on it tightly. This list was ongoing and definitely a joke I don't think was really meant to be a secret, so I didn't fight that hard to keep the notebook in my possession. She slid it from my desk and set it on hers.

I watched her shoulders shake as she tried to laugh without making a sound. She never even looked up to get permission from me to turn the page before she flipped through and found another one of our lists. TOP TEN 31-FLAVOR FLAVORS.

I rested my elbow on my desk so I could rest my head on my hand and watch her as she browsed through the lists I hadn't moved into my desk drawer yet.

"I didn't know you guys still made these," she whispered when she found a list titled TOP TEN REASONS HENRY WOULD MAKE A PERFECT COMIC BOOK VILLAIN dated the weekend we'd all gone to the beach together.

I smiled and nodded.

Nisha closed the notebook and set it back on my desk. "If this class gets any more boring, you and I could make a list of the top ten reasons why we're going to get an F on the final, starting with how hard it is to pay attention to the lectures."

nineteen

JUDE HAD PICKED me up on time and we'd managed to get out of my house with only a few awkward minutes of meeting my parents. We were sitting in the back of the Italian restaurant waiting for our drinks to arrive. I found myself nervously playing with the hem of the tablecloth that lay in my lap. "So," Jude began, "have you decided where to go once we graduate?"

"I'm going to UCLA. What about you?"

Jude took a small piece of bread from the basket and then held it over my plate, offering me a piece. I shook my head. Better not. My numbers had been crazy and bread was a hard thing to account for, especially since I knew I'd be eating pasta and having to take a wild guess about how many carbs it might have.

"I'm going to stay here and go to community college. I'm not sure what I want to study yet. I figure, why waste the money if I don't know what direction I want to go in." He dipped the bread into the oil and vinegar mix on the table. "Do you already know what you want to do?"

"I want to be a journalist."

"That's cool. What kind of stories do you want to cover? Sports? Entertainment? World news?"

"I'm not sure yet. I just know that I love writing and hate the idea of office jobs. I want to go out in the field and spend my day talking to people. I know I'll have to work behind a desk too, but at least it would be worth it if I didn't have to do it every day." The waitress arrived with our food and I felt a little nervous and shy about bringing out my kit. This was one of those moments I always dreaded when I ate with someone new. Most people just ignored it, but every so often someone would make a comment about how testing myself was "freaky" or "gross."

Clearly I shouldn't have been worried about Jude, though.

"How long have you been diabetic?" he asked nicely and with genuine curiosity after I tested myself.

"Since fourth grade." I picked up a fork and began to twirl my pasta.

"That must have been hard. I would hide from shots until I was thirteen."

I laughed. "They made me use syringes for a year before they let me get a pump. My doctor wanted everyone to learn how to take care of me without it first. Pumps do all the calculations for you, so my doctor thought it was important that we knew how to do them without it so we had a better understanding of how the insulin was working in my body to bring down my blood sugar as we figured out my dosing. He said we needed to know how to do injections in case there was ever a problem with my pump. I cried a bit at first, but after a while it was so quick I barely had time to make any fuss." I took a bite of the delicious fettuccini Alfredo.

"If I had known you back then I would have thought you were some sort of superhero." He cut a bite of his lasagna and raised it to his mouth. "To be a kid and get a shot without crying . . ." His eyes went wide and he let out a small whistle. It made me laugh and feel proud of the brave little girl I'd been forced to be. It also made me happy I was on this date with Jude. Talking to him felt so effortless. His smile was cute too.

"I saw you leaving school early Wednesday with Antonio

and Kenji. Do you guys have a zero period and no sixth?"

"Surf. We have to be at the beach at six in the morning on Tuesdays and Thursdays. We surf until about eight and then head home to shower up and get to school. It counts as our PE and zero period. Sometimes if the waves are good we stay past eight and just rinse off in the freshwater showers they have near the strand. If it looks like the waves are going to be good after school we'll head back down too." He seemed at ease discussing surfing. I could tell he loved it.

"I saw you riding your skateboard a few times as I was driving, but I didn't know you surfed too. How long have you been doing that?"

"It feels like I've been surfing forever. My dad taught me. He surfs as a way to relax before big surgeries. I think the first time he put me on a board I was five. I'm not really sure when I started doing it by myself but I know we have pictures of a family vacation in Hawaii and I can't be more than maybe seven years old and I'm riding a wave by myself." He shrugged like it was not a big deal. To me it was so impressive I had stopped eating while listening to him talk.

"Wow, that's incredible. I wasn't doing anything like that when I was seven." I laughed. "I don't think I could even do that now."

"I could teach you," he said quickly. I could hear in his voice how eager he was for me to accept his offer. It made me grin and my cheeks felt warm.

"Okay, but I should warn you that I've never been on a surfboard. I've read about it, though." I bit my lip, praying he didn't think girls who read instead of surfed weren't worth a second date because I knew right then I wanted a second one.

"I have some great books about surfing. Do you like to read fiction or nonfiction?" he asked. In his excitement he didn't even wait for me to answer. "I have a book about the woman who was bitten by a great white shark while surfing, but maybe you should hold off on it until you've gained some confidence on your board."

"So you surf and read?" I teased.

"Yeah, I always have. I guess it's because of how I grew up. My parents got divorced when I was nine. My mom lives about two hours from here now, so when it's her time with me it's a long trip back and forth. I don't have to go very often, but reading was something they both encouraged to help pass the time. She's a teacher, so between her and my dad's love for knowledge, if my head wasn't in the ocean, it was in a book." He held his fork above his dinner. "I guess it's still that way."

"Two hours away?" I asked. "That must be rough."

"It probably would be if it was inland," he answered with a knowing grin, "but she moved down the coast. I kind of get the best of both worlds now. I get to surf here and right outside of San Diego. Doesn't get much better than that."

I realized that talking to Jude was easy. He was friendly and interesting, and the more I talked with him, the more I wanted the night to continue. We lingered over dessert, discussing everything from the piece I had written in the school paper about the unequal funding the male and female sports teams received to the time that I had accidentally kicked a hornets' nest and gotten ten stings. He asked me questions about myself that I hadn't really thought anyone would be interested in, and I realized we had so much in common that the conversation never felt stilted. I really liked him. He didn't make my heart beat as quickly as it did when Nolan touched me or smiled a particular way, but it did speed up a little as we walked up to my door.

"Thank you for going out with me," he said when we stopped on my porch. I turned to him and smiled.

"Thanks for taking me. I had a good time." Never mind what I said earlier about my heart; it seemed to jump the second I realized we were going to kiss. It pounded against my ribs and made my head feel dizzy. The tense moment built up around us. Finally, he leaned forward and kissed my lips. It wasn't as intense as my last kiss, but it was nice. His lips were soft against mine and he even put his hand to the side of my head, causing a warm rush to race through my body.

When the kiss finally broke, he took a step back with a smile on his face. "I'd like to take you out again."

"I'd like that too," I answered honestly, my heart still pumping a little quicker than it usually did. He nodded and then turned around. I watched as he moved toward his car, parked at the curb. He turned his head to look at me one more time and I could clearly see his smile even though it was dark outside.

twenty

SATURDAY MORNING NISHA, Regan, and I went to get breakfast at our favorite coffee shop so they could get all the details of my date with Jude at the same time. They swore they weren't jealous of each other, but when it all came down to it, they would admit that they couldn't stand being the last to hear the gossip.

"So he actually watches *The Bachelor* and wasn't just saying that to have something to talk to you about?" Nisha asked.

"There's no way he doesn't watch it. He knows too much. Not just about this season either. He knows the names of all the past contestants and had a pretty convincing theory about who the bachelor is going to pick this time." I smiled, remembering how fun it had been to debate our theories.

"Did you hold hands?" Regan asked as the waitress refilled her water.

"He held my hand for the ride back to my house," I tell them, remembering the way it had felt to feel his warm hand in mine. He'd held it the right way and I'd had to look out the window so he couldn't catch me smiling so widely all my teeth were probably showing.

"I just can't believe it," Nisha said. "It's going to be hard to get used to." She took a sip of her drink. "We've never seen you with any boy other than Nolan. When you and Jude start hanging out it's going to make everyone do a double take the first time they see you together."

"It had to happen sometime," Regan said. "I think now is good." She smiled and popped a strawberry from her small bowl of fruit into her mouth. "I can tell you're happy just by the look on your face."

"I can't believe how much is changing this year," Nisha said as she watched the waves crash beyond the strand. "We're graduating in a few months and we've all picked different colleges. Declan and I won't even be in the same state." Her voice trailed off for a moment, and I wondered if she was lost in the idea of her boyfriend being hundreds of miles away.

"You'll get through it," I told her. "You both promised to come home for winter break."

"It's not just us; Regan is going to get her girl, Nolan found Erin, and you and Jude make the cutest couple. It's wonderful we're all happy in this moment, but you have to admit the timing is terrible." She laughed, and I could tell she was trying to be strong when her heart was breaking.

"Don't go there, Nisha," Regan warned lovingly. "You're going to be so worried about having to leave each other that you won't enjoy the time you have left together."

Nisha nodded. She seemed to understand that logic. "Graduation is making me sentimental, I guess," she confessed, pushing her sunglasses up and wiping a tear off her cheek. "But I have to be honest," she said casually, "a little part of me always thought you and Nolan would end up together. I know it's silly—you guys have told us all a million times you're only friends—but the romantic in me wanted you to fall in love because you're just so perfect for each other and you have all that history." She smiled at me, as if to express that she knew the idea was nonsense. I almost told her that I'd wanted the same thing, but what good would it have done? She was right to call it a fantasy and it was time to grow up and look to the future.

■ ■ ■

That afternoon, after Nolan's game, we headed to Target so we could grab the supplies we'd need for the campout. His parents were actually going to be out of town, visiting some old friends from high school, so they'd left him money so that he could get food for his brothers and some snacks for us. We entered Target through the sliding glass doors and I noticed the way Nolan attracted attention as he clicked along the linoleum in his cleats. His baseball pants were stained from where he had sat on the dirty bench inside the dugout and his hair was wet with sweat and slightly wavy as it hung down by his eyes. Even just warming up had taken its toll, and he'd had to ice his shoulder the rest of the game. Sitting out the game on doctor's orders was hard for him, especially on such a sunny perfect day for baseball.

"What?" he asked when he caught me smiling.

"You're a mess. It's embarrassing." I was joking, of course, and he knew it. I didn't get embarrassed easily, and definitely not in front of him.

"What, this?" He swept his arm down the length of his body. I tried to hide my smile. "This is not embarrassing."

"It's not?" I shook my head slightly. "Because I think it's a little embarrassing. You have an ice pack wrapped around your arm."

"No," he said confidently. "That's not embarrassing. Now,

if I did something like this . . ." He started dancing in the middle of the aisle. Not some smooth dance that you'd see in a romance movie, but more like a robot having a malfunction. He added in facial expressions to make sure I was completely hysterical with laughter. A woman with her small children passed us by and the kids pointed at him and smiled. She tried hard to scold them for pointing and moved away from Nolan as quickly as possible. It only egged him on more. He added some sort of a shuffle, which had the kids giggling.

Just as quickly as he had started, he stopped. "Now that was embarrassing."

"Right. I've got it now." I followed him over to the grocery section of the store and we began throwing items into the cart like people who had just descended from a twelve-month hike of Everest. With our cart full of everything we probably shouldn't be eating, we headed over to the camping section to get my sleeping bag.

"This one, of course," he said as he reached for a tiny Disney sleeping bag.

"I think I might be ready for a big-girl sleeping bag. Maybe this one." I tossed in a flannel sleeping bag and pulled the cart down to the end of the aisle, where all the insect repellents were. I tossed in some bug spray and was about to leave when Nolan swiped a bunch of citronella candles into the cart.

"You can never be too careful," he explained as an older man checking out small portable stoves gave him a dirty look when the candles clanked and clattered into our overstuffed cart.

I slipped into the next aisle and tried to contain my laughter. Nolan followed and did the same. He marched around, mocking the way the old man had balked at us and then turned and marched to the other end of the aisle, as if we had somehow contaminated his shopping area.

It took a few minutes of not looking at each other to get our silent laughing under control, and when we finally left that aisle, my cheeks were sore from smiling and my eyes were red with happy tears. We made a funny pair at the checkout: a messy, broken baseball player and a girl who looked like she'd been crying while still smiling like a loon.

twenty-one

THE SUN WAS just about to set when I opened the small gate that led to his yard. I had a bag packed with a few items I might need. Nolan was already outside, sitting on top of a big blanket. I felt my heart flutter in my chest and my pulse quicken when I took in the sight before me. He had lit every single candle and more. I'm not sure when he even got all of them.

I slowly made my way over to the small circle of fire and stepped inside, sitting cross-legged beside him. "You think this will keep the mosquitoes away?" he asked, staring out across the yard as if the bug apocalypse was on its way.

"It's gonna be close, but I think we have one up on them." I smiled and then leaned back on my hands. "What's first on the agenda?" When we were younger we'd play hide-and-seek or tag while we waited for it to get dark, and then we'd start in on all the snacks we'd brought out. As we got a little older, I'd bring a book and he'd bring a graphic novel and we'd read until the light of the day was gone.

"I of course brought the best book of all time out with me tonight. I also brought snacks and a card game. What are you in the mood for?" Nolan asked.

Before I could answer, the back door slammed and Seth made his way into the backyard toward us. "Dude, I'm going to Bonnie's house. Hey, Mackenzie," he said almost like an afterthought.

"Do Mom and Dad know that you're going over there?" Nolan asked.

"Nope. And they aren't going to."

"Not cool. I'm not keeping your secret!" he yelled after him.

"Yes, you are," Seth tossed back as he headed out the gate.

"I'm not keeping his secret," Nolan said almost to himself.

"Yes, you are." I scooted down farther and folded my arms behind my head. "You keep every secret your brothers tell you. Stop pretending that you're suddenly righteous."

Nolan moved down and copied my position. "My parents don't think it's a good idea that they're so serious. They're worried that they're both impulsive and their relationship is getting in the way of his schoolwork." He said it in the same tone I imagine his parents used.

"What do you think?"

"I think he's going to do whatever he wants to do no matter what my parents think about it. He's never been one to follow directions. My parents know that. I think that's why they are so strict with him. They put down a boundary knowing that he is going to cross that line just a bit. They're not stupid; they know where to draw the line so that the real line won't be crossed."

The sun sank farther and the darkness began to creep into the yard. "Would your parents make the same rules for you if you got serious with a girl?" I turned my head so that I could look at him as he stared up into the sky.

"It's complicated," he answered after a pause. I waited for him to elaborate but he didn't.

"I thought parents were supposed to keep the rules the same for all of their kids. Why would you be treated different?"

"That's what society tells you. Parents should parent all children the same way, but not all kids are the same. My parents make things fair, and making things fair doesn't necessarily mean treating us the same."

I leaned up onto my side, turning to him and propping my head on my hand. "What do you mean?"

He turned to me, rolling onto his side too so that we were facing each other. "I don't have trouble with school, right?" I nodded, agreeing with him. "Seth does. He doesn't study well and can't pay attention. If things were the same, Seth and I would have the same rules about our grades. If that were true, it wouldn't be fair. Like if my parents didn't make him work with a tutor, he'd probably fail English. What's fair is that we both have the same opportunities, not the same expectations and goals."

"I don't understand how that would relate to you dating someone. I've never heard them give you rules about who you're allowed to date and who you aren't." I tucked my hair behind my ear when the wind sent it flying into my face.

"I have rules." He smiled and I felt a little left out. How come he had never told me about them?

"What rules do they have for you?"

"What rules do your parents have for you?" he countered. Fine, I'd bite.

"I guess that depends on if we're talking about written or unwritten rules." I thought he would ask me to clarify, but he only smiled. "The written rules would be my curfew, where he's taking me, and of course how old he would be."

"And the unwritten rules?"

"No criminals. No sex. No eloping. Let me think." I looked up to the sky, trying to gather my thoughts. "No one who wouldn't respect me or them." I looked back to him. "Now your turn. Written first."

"Curfew, distance, budget, and sex."

"Sex is something you guys talk about? You haven't mentioned discussing sex with your parents since your dad gave you that awkward talk in fifth grade." I laughed softly.

"That was really terrible, wasn't it?" He had told me about it the night it had happened. He said his dad had explained everything to him in a rush of words and quick hand gestures. He'd been totally embarrassed and swore it was all going to traumatize him forever. "Yes, in my house we talk about sex. I am not to be having any of it." He laughed.

"Okay, the unwritten ones." His face fell for a minute. There was a seriousness that seemed odd in this conversation. I almost took it back, but he tapped my nose and answered.

"Respect boundaries. Be a good example for your brothers. And don't ruin what years have built."

"What years have built? You mean reputations?"

"Something like that," he said with a noncommittal shrug

of one shoulder. "Are you ready to get this campout started?"

My lips curled with a smile and I sat up, unsure what I would need to do to make that happen. "What's up first?" I asked as Nolan reached into his bag.

"*Scary Stories to Tell in the Dark*!" He pulled out a tattered old book that instantly transported me back to our childhood. We must have read that thing a million times since he had gotten it one year for his birthday. We brought it to every campout and every family vacation. It had been a long time since I'd seen it and it made me wonder how we ever got out of the habit of having it around.

"I've missed that book."

"Well, apparently we scared the crap out of my brother with it because I had to search the whole house for it and only found it when he admitted he'd put it under his bed after the trip to San Diego. Remember when we had him convinced a corpse was coming after him because he thought Seth had something of his?"

"I do remember that!" I laughed. "We got in so much trouble for that. My mom told me I was going to be grounded until he wasn't afraid to sleep in his own room anymore."

"Two weeks," Nolan says. "It took him two weeks to forget about it." He set the book between us and then reached into his bag for a flashlight. We probably could have seen the words with just the candlelight, but it was always more scary to tell a story with a bright light shining up eerily from your chin.

We took turns reading the old stories, mostly laughing instead of being scared. It's weird what a few years had done to change the emotions each story provoked. I wasn't terrified out of my mind. It was more like I was wrapped up warm in the comfort of nostalgia. Telling those stories with Nolan would always be some of my favorite memories.

When we'd gotten through the best stories, I asked, "How about I check myself so we can have some snacks?" I pulled my bag closer and retrieved my kit. He kept the light on me so I could read my number. He used to do that for me when we were kids too.

When I had my kit tucked back away, he pulled out graham crackers, marshmallows, a Hershey bar, and two long wooden sticks. "S'mores?" I asked as he set a small kerosene burner between us.

"Of course. I don't think we've ever camped without them." He lit the burner and stabbed a marshmallow with the wooden stick. He handed it over to me across the flame and then prepared one for himself. We held them over the small flame until they bubbled and the edges were barely brown. Then he helped me squish the pieces together, and I wasn't sure I'd ever eaten a s'more more delicious than that one.

"What's your best guess?" I asked when I finished the treat. I reached for my pump and pulled up the menu.

"Twenty-three." He answered too quickly for it to have been a guess.

"You looked that up, didn't you?" I typed in the carbs and administered the insulin.

"Maybe," he answered, stuffing the last bite into his mouth.

"Aren't you looking forward to when we go to college and you can have friendships that won't involve math?" I licked a little chocolate off my finger.

"I guess I never really thought about it." He looked at me a minute. "It's not like it makes being friends with you difficult. You don't ask me to count your carbs or help in any way."

"I know, but you always do." I folded my hands together and set them in my lap, unsure what I should be doing with them while we talked.

"Are you looking forward to making new friends who won't know as much as I do about it so they won't worry?"

It was the first time he'd ever really admitted to worrying about me. I knew that already, of course, but I guess hearing him say it out loud stung a little. I hated the idea that I was someone anyone had to worry about, let alone Nolan.

"Do you ever wish it was different between us? How

tangled up in each other's lives we are, I mean."

"No," he answered right away. "I like it the way it is. You shouldn't try to fix what isn't broken. I worry about you because I care about you. I like that I know about diabetes so that I can help you. I think it would be far scarier if I didn't understand it. After all, could I ever really understand you if I knew nothing about what you were living with?"

"But what if we had just met later in life?" I untangled my hands and then tangled them back up again. "Maybe we would have just bumped into each other at school or while we were out with other friends. Could you imagine how different everything would be if you hadn't saved my life that day—if it had been someone else?" It was something I had been tossing around in my head for years. I needed to know if he'd ever done that too. If we had not been friends first, would he have wanted to get to know me in another way?

"What if we were just acquaintances or kids who sat next to each other in class? Maybe we would never figure out how good we are as friends. Then I wouldn't know that you get forgetful when you're low, or that your middle finger hurts less to prick than the others. I wouldn't know that you get a little sweaty and your thoughts tend to race when your blood sugar is high. I wouldn't know that you hate when you have to change your pump site or that you get super excited but really stressed when it's time to pick a new pump. If we had met some other time, maybe I wouldn't know anything about that part of you. I think I would have wanted to have found all of that out. I think we were destined to be friends."

I released my hands, feeling the weight of a very heavy sadness rest on my chest. I wanted him to know about me and I wanted to know everything about him too. Even if we had met much later than we did, I also believed the result would be the same. It wasn't really about when or how we met; it was about who he was as a person and the Nolan I knew loved and cared about me. All roads would always lead to us becoming friends.

twenty-two

SUNDAY WAS ROUGH since we had stayed up most of the night talking and laughing like we always did. We waited until the last possible moment to blow out the candles and then Nolan made sure I was zipped up and tucked in as tight as possible in my sleeping bag so the bugs couldn't get to me. It was peaceful as we listened to the hum of cars passing in the distance and gazed at the stars above us. Sometimes when the world feels like it's spinning too fast and the years are slipping by too quickly, it just takes a night in the dark beneath the stars to feel it all slow down again.

What I didn't expect was to be woken up by his automatic sprinklers at six in the morning. I had been dreaming about shopping for shoes when I became aware of a *tsk, tsk, tsk* in the background. Then the sound had grown more insistent and the shoes I'd been trying on felt wet. Really wet. Finally my name being called in a panic caused me to wake up and realize we were right in the center of the yard, which was currently being soaked by his sprinklers.

Nolan was trying hard to call to me as he climbed out of his soggy sleeping bag. He started tucking anything he could into it before dragging it off the grass and onto the deck. I jumped from my bag and followed, squealing as one particularly vindictive sprinkler followed me, spraying harshly as I tried to escape its wrath.

After the sprinklers finally shut off and I was safe to make my way across the yard to my house, I gave Nolan a hug and told him we'd catch up later after a long nap. I made the trek home and left my wet clothes in the bathroom when I snuggled into a fresh pair of pajamas and headed to my warm, bug-free bed.

When I woke up a few hours later, I pulled our napkin out of my kit and reread each item again. Last night had been perfect and I was already looking forward to checking the next thing off the list.

■ ■ ■

On Monday, Nolan had an MRI. It took a few days for his doctor to get the results, but by the time we were sitting in his follow-up appointment on Friday, he was able to learn he had not torn his shoulder, but there was a lot of inflammation around his old injury. It didn't require more surgery, but it did require him to take it easy until it could heal. He was already feeling much better, but the doctor gave him a shot of steroids right into his shoulder and then urged him to keep it iced and not pitch for at least one more week. I knew out of all the information he was given, not being able to pitch would be the hardest to receive.

Henry was one of the team's other pitchers. He and Nolan often battled for the position, which led to a lot of rivalry and ugly words tossed between them. When Nolan told the coach on Friday what his doctor had told him that morning, Henry had gloated about his increased time on the pitching mound due to Nolan's absence. He might have played nice when we were all at the beach, but now the gloves were off. He thought he was God's gift to everyone and that we should all be so honored he was playing baseball at our school. His parents jumped right in and were of course the president and vice president of his hypothetical fan club. You know the type; the ones who insisted their child be played above others and talked about his future in the major leagues.

Nolan's parents had tried to make friends with them at the beginning of their freshman year, but couldn't stand listening to them talk about their kid nonstop, all while putting Nolan's playing down. The friendship had ended before the season had, and there was a clear line drawn in the bleachers that both families knew not to cross. It was just best if the two didn't mix together.

In a matter of a few hours, social media was blowing up with the news of Nolan's injury. Henry was telling everyone about it, and to make things worse, he was exaggerating the extent of it and causing a bit of hysteria among Nolan's friends and fans of the school's baseball team. Stories about multiple surgeries, career-ending injuries, and metal pins were circulating quicker than Nolan could refute them. His parents made the decision to call USC and keep them in the loop so that they would not become aware of his injury over the social media sites.

I was watching my friend's frustration build and build without any outlet or release because of the large spotlight on him and the consequences he'd suffer if he acted out in any way. Henry knew Nolan couldn't retaliate without risking his scholarship or facing other consequences with the team.

I was sitting on my kitchen counter again late Friday night, sipping on a juice before heading to bed. Nolan was pacing, irritated that he had to give the starting pitcher position up to Henry for a game he'd really been looking forward to pitching in. I knew better than to say anything and just let him vent. He stopped midsentence when he discovered the foil-covered pan of brownies my mom had made earlier. "Brownies?" he asked, his voice sounding hopeful for the first time all day.

"Yup. They're even iced." I jumped down off the counter and pulled back the corner of the foil.

He held his hand over his heart. "I love your mom."

I grabbed us two paper plates from the cupboard and two forks and a knife from the drawer beneath the pan. I cut us each a piece of brownie and then leaned back and rested against the counter as I ate the gooey deliciousness.

"Do you think he'll go to bed early tonight?" I asked, my words muffled a little due to the thick chocolate. I looked down at my pump, remembering I'd need to cover myself, but my hands were full. Nolan reached for my pump with one hand while balancing his brownie plate with the other. He typed in something and turned it toward me so I could check the amount of carbs he had guessed for the brownie I was eating. When I nodded, he administered the insulin and tucked my pump back into my pouch.

"Who?"

"Henry. Do you think he'll go to bed early tonight so

that he'll be rested for the game?" I cut another bite and slid it between my teeth.

"Probably." Nolan cut a much bigger piece of his brownie and scooped it into his mouth.

"Then let's cross another thing off our list while you get your vengeance. It kind of kills two birds with one stone." I finished off my brownie and rinsed my fork in the sink.

"That's brilliant." He moved in behind me and rinsed his fork too. We put both of them into the dishwasher and tossed our paper plates in the trash.

I looked over Nolan's light gray shorts and bright white shirt. What he was wearing would give us away for sure. "Let's change and meet up in front in fifteen minutes. We have to go get the toilet paper and then pretend to be going to sleep."

"I like your thinking," he said, tapping my head lightly with his finger. "I'll see you outside."

It was just after midnight when I managed to quietly escape my house. I was dressed completely in black except for my shoes. I had my hood up over my hair and was standing by his truck when I heard him step up behind me. He was dressed in dark jeans, a dark hoodie, and a pair of dark skate shoes.

He put his finger over his lips to signal for me to be quiet and I nodded. He grabbed my hand and tugged me around to the driver's side. As quietly as possible, he opened the door and whispered for me to get inside.

"Put it in neutral and keep your foot on the brake until I start pushing. I'm going to push it down the driveway and I need you to steer it out and onto the road." He put the keys in my lap and then closed the door the best he could without letting it shut completely and make a sound. I put my foot on the brake and turned the key to on. Next, I shifted the truck into neutral and lifted my foot from the brake. I began to roll down the driveway and worked hard to steer the truck straight onto the road. When I was fully out and facing the right way, Nolan moved to the back of the truck and pushed us the length of four houses with his good shoulder pressed against the tailgate.

"Okay, scoot over," he instructed as he opened my door. I climbed across the center and into my seat, laughing a little at how much toilet paper was in the back of his truck.

When we pulled onto Henry's street, Nolan cut the lights and parked a few houses away. We waited and watched for a minute, but there was no activity happening inside. The lights were all off and there hadn't been a car driving down the small street since we'd been there. "Let's start with the tree," Nolan whispered across the cab. We slipped out of the truck, letting the doors slowly close without latching. Nolan grabbed one of our large cases of toilet paper and we left the other two in the bed of his truck. There had to be over one hundred rolls.

In Henry's yard, Nolan got his roll out before I could and took a few steps back from where we had set the case at the trunk of the tall tree in front of the house. He let a long strand of paper unravel before throwing the roll up into the tree and watching the white paper stream down toward the ground.

I got my roll out and joined him, tossing it over the branch and then chasing it when it bounced into the street. Within twenty minutes, long white strands hung everywhere there used to be open space. I couldn't even see Nolan anymore; he was lost somewhere on the other side of the toilet paper jungle. After another fifteen minutes, it passed up beautiful and headed straight for amazing. Roll after roll of toilet paper was flung into the tree, and the result was nothing less than spectacular.

Once we were finished with the tree, we wrapped the bushes like we were sending them somewhere far away. Not one leaf stuck out from beneath our strands. We still had some rolls left, so we sat down in the center of his lawn and began ripping the paper directly from the roll, creating short strands of paper and then tossing them over our heads onto the lawn. It didn't take long for the entire front landscaping to be covered in a layer of toilet paper snow. Various lengths and thicknesses added to the natural look of the paper as it dipped with the terrain beneath it and rose with the rocks and small hedges.

I was busy tossing a handful when lights flashed from the end of the street. Nolan and I ran for cover, tucking ourselves between Henry's house and the neighbors'. The car slowed to a stop in front and my heart jumped up and into my throat. We'd never been this close to being caught before and I suddenly worried we would be in a lot of trouble. Just when I thought I might actually pass out from the adrenaline coursing through my system, I heard a young voice say, "That's impressive" from the car and then the sound of a phone taking pictures. Another voice from the car said, "He deserves it. Asshole."

Once the car drove off, Nolan pulled me up to my feet and we ran back to his truck. I took one last look at our masterpiece as we drove past it and down to the other end of the street. In the stillness of the dark night, I realized even though we might never TP another house together, we'd always be there to help right the wrongs that would happen in our lives. Look at what the two of us could do with love, friendship, and a few cases of toilet paper.

twenty-three

I FELT THE sharp stick of the lancet as my eyes fluttered open early the next day. My mom was standing above me, testing my blood sugar without her glasses. A few nights a week my mom would wake up with what she referred to as an "intuitive feeling," and she wouldn't be able to go back to sleep until she knew my blood sugar was okay. It was always funny to watch her try to squint so she could see the small print on my meter. I sat up and startled her, but she didn't scream. She just held her hand over her heart as I held my hand out for her to put the meter in.

"Why are you sleeping in your hoodie?" she asked as

she sat down next to me on my bed.

"I was cold. One thirty." I handed her back the meter and tucked myself back into the covers. I watched through one eye as she tried to find the door to the hallway in the darkness. When she was close, she kicked my discarded shoe and I saw it fly a bit and then land with the sole up on the empty plastic wrap from the large case of toilet paper. Staring right at me was a square of dewy wet toilet paper. My mom glanced down to investigate, picking it up and looking at it closely. She turned back to me but I shut my eyes and pretended to be sleeping.

I woke up a couple of hours later, and rushed to get dressed before Nisha, Regan, Nolan, and Declan came over for lunch. My parents were out buying my dad a new suit for work so we decided to order a pizza and eat it in the living room while watching TV. I was settling onto the couch with a slice when my phone chimed.

JUDE: Are you free later? Maybe we could grab a burger.

I smiled when I saw it was Jude. I snuck a look at Nolan, my feelings warring inside my heart. I didn't think it would ever be possible to be interested in anyone else, but Jude showed me I could be. Maybe it wouldn't be as powerful, but could I really expect that with all the history I had with Nolan?

ME: A burger sounds good. I'm going to Nolan's game. You could come with me.

JUDE: Sounds good. I'll meet you there. What time?

ME: 5pm.

JUDE: See you soon.

When I looked up from my phone, everyone was watching me. Declan smiled sweetly. "Are you talking to Jude?"

"Yes. How did you know?" I asked.

"Because I've never seen you smile like that when you're talking to anyone else." He tossed a napkin at me and I knew my cheeks were red.

"He wanted to grab a burger tonight so I invited him to come watch Nolan's game before and then go out to eat after." I felt nervous suddenly. Not really about the date, but about talking to everyone about it.

"Cool. It seems like he's into you," Declan said, stretching his arm behind Nisha's back as they lounged on the couch.

"We'll see. Tonight will only be our second date," I told him.

"True, but you invited him to a school event where everyone could see you together. That's a big deal."

I hadn't really thought about that and I felt the blood drain from my face. Nolan chuckled. "Stop. Don't freak out. Declan was just pointing out that people might see you guys together and he said yes. He wouldn't have done that if he wasn't really into you."

I blew out a breath. "Okay. Right. I won't freak out." I giggled nervously. "I just really like him."

"I'm happy for you, Sugar." Nolan smiled at me, but there was something that didn't quite feel right about it.

"What's going on with you?" I asked. I nudged his thigh with my foot. "You seem a little off your game. Are you worried about your shoulder?"

"Yes and no." He set his plate down on the coffee table and leaned back against the couch, stretching his strong arm along the back. "I'm worried about my shoulder, but that's not all."

"Erin?"

He nodded. "She's coming to the game tonight. I'm hoping she'll sit by you. I know I can't force a friendship between you guys just to make my life easier"—he smiled—"but you're both really cool girls, and I think if you got to know each other more, there'd be potential for a real friendship."

"If she is what makes you happy, then I'll do whatever you ask." I patted his arm with my hand.

"I think she is."

■ ■ ■

Erin came to the game a little late. I waved her over to our section. "Hey, Erin. Nice to see you."

"Hey. Good to see you too." She brushed off the bench next to me and sat down. "I read your article about teen refs in Little League," she told me.

My article had come out last week and the student body seemed to be enjoying reading about the crazy experiences their peers had while doing their jobs. "Thank you. What did you think?" I put my feet up on the bench in front of me and leaned forward so I could watch Nolan in the outfield.

"I think you did a great job. We don't ever have teen refs for volleyball, but I've seen parents yell at the adult coaches so terribly that they've been told they had to leave the gym and not come back. I can't imagine ever being that mad." She pulled a water bottle out of her purse and twisted off the cap. After taking a sip, she spun around and said hi to our parents. They said hi back and gave her a few small waves.

"Me either," I agreed.

The batter hit a high one out to right field and Nolan caught it. He threw it to second, making a double play. The crowd cheered, of course, happy he'd tied up the inning without letting anyone score. As he ran back to the dugout, his eyes met mine. He smiled at me and then looked at Erin. She waved to him and he lifted his chin in that way the players did to say hello to people in the stands.

"Have you noticed Nolan acting different lately?" Erin asked, her eyes still trained on where he'd disappeared into the dugout.

"Pain medication makes him act weird," I told her.

"I don't know," she said, "I think it might be something else."

I thought about the last few days. Nolan had been different, but I would describe it as being more vulnerable, and I wasn't sure that's what Erin was getting at. "What do you mean?" I asked.

She sat back, lifting her feet up onto the seat below us. "He seems preoccupied with something."

For a second I'd let myself imagine it was our kiss. Nolan's easy dismissal of something so special to me had left a wound I'd been pretending I didn't have. I had no one to share it with, no one I could talk to about it, and the person I would normally have gone to first was the one who had inflicted it. I wanted him to be drowning in the water from the dam we had broken that night just like me, but every minute I was with him, all I could see was how easy it was for him to have forgotten all about it.

Erin's voice brought me out of my thoughts. "I think he's really stressing about his scholarship."

It made much more sense, and I nodded when she

turned to look at me because I worried my voice might not have been strong enough to answer her out loud. It was so interesting to think that I had worried Nolan might regret the kiss when in the end it was me who was grappling with my own regret for crossing the line that night.

Nolan came up to bat three batters later and hit a double. I saw Jude far out in the field, making his way toward me. He had his hands in his pockets as he walked along the back of the dugout and around to where Erin and I were sitting behind home plate. He waved to my parents and then took the seat right next to me.

"Hey, Jude." I greeted him with a hug. It was different from the ones Nolan gave me, but I liked it. It was not complicated, and in that moment especially, I could appreciate that.

"Hi, Erin," he said over my shoulder when he saw her sitting beside me.

"Hi." She smiled and looked relieved. I don't think she was even aware of it, but I'm sure the more she saw me with another guy, the easier it was for her to trust that I was not romantically interested in Nolan.

I loved watching Nolan play, but I had to admit that watching the game with Erin and Jude made the whole thing even better. It took a few innings to get comfortable, but by the time the game was over, we were all talking and joking like we'd been friends all year.

After the game, I walked Erin down to the place where I knew she could find Nolan. It was usually where I stood after the games, but today I had other plans. I invited her and Nolan to meet up with Jude and me for dinner after he'd changed out of his uniform. She gave me a hug and thanked me for keeping her company during the game. We left her there, smiling while she waited for him to come out.

Jude and I walked side by side until we reached the far gate of the school and the parking lot. As we stepped off the curb to cross the street, he reached down and put his hand in mine. Each finger was resting in between just like they should. I knew I was smiling when we reached his car, but he was too, so it wasn't that embarrassing. We climbed into his older Mustang and pulled out of the parking lot. I texted my parents that I was getting a bite to eat with Jude as we waited for the light.

The traffic on the street was backed up as the guests, parents, and players of both teams spilled off the fields and into the street. I looked up when I heard the rumble of Nolan's truck. The world seemed to slow down for just a moment as we passed him while he waited to turn off one of the small residential streets. Our eyes met and immediately he gave me a small nod, as if to say he was happy I was leaving with Jude. I waved, but it was a very delayed response, and I wasn't even sure if he'd seen it. When my hand landed back on my lap, Jude reached for it.

Steve's was a family-owned burger place close to campus, so it was pretty crowded with the families from the game by the time we stepped through the doors. We waited in line and I couldn't help but notice the way kids from school seemed to do a double take when they walked past or saw us from their booths. I didn't know if they were surprised I wasn't with Nolan, or if it was because I was with Jude. I felt a little shaky, probably because of my nerves and the excitement of spending more time with Jude. The line had stretched outside the doors, and by the time we reached the counter I was having trouble reading the menu. I tried squinting my eyes but it didn't help so I just ordered a burger, fries with ranch dressing, and a diet soda. I knew my blood sugar had to be low, but since we were going to be at our table soon, I decided to wait until then to get my kit out. Jude paid for our order and I thanked him as we made our way to the last empty table. Before we reached our destination, a guy that I recognized from math class stopped us to chat about the game. I started to feel like my legs were getting a bit wobbly. I wanted to check myself, but it just seemed odd to pull out my kit in the middle of a conversation. I checked my purse quickly for a snack that could bring my blood sugar up, but I had forgotten to refill it after the last time I'd used it. I waited, hoping to catch Jude's eye and signal that I needed to move a little quicker to the table.

Everything happened so fast. I took a step toward the table, but stumbled like I was drunk and grabbed on to a different table instead. I felt my eyes starting to shut as I tried hard to hold myself up on my own feet. I wanted to move my arm to get a better grip, but when I tried it felt like it had been asleep for hours. I could see it moving, knocking ketchup and napkins off the table. I was no longer in control of my limbs. As I slipped down to the floor, unable to stand any longer, I saw the horrified and helpless look on Jude's face.

"Zie!" I heard Nolan's voice as if it were at the bottom of an echo chamber. I closed my eyes, too tired to keep them open any longer. His voice was so far away. I felt something clamp around my mouth, prying open my lips. "Chew," he instructed, and I tried, but my tongue just felt so big in my small mouth. He moved my jaw for me and I had to swallow or I was going to choke. I felt the tiny crystals of sugar on my tongue as he emptied tiny envelope after tiny envelope into my clumsy mouth.

He sat on the floor next to me, my head propped up in his lap and his hand stroking my hair as I regained my abilities. There was a big circle of people around us and I knew

I was deeply embarrassed, but I just couldn't feel it through the gratefulness that filled my heart when his eyes looked down into mine. I moved my heavy arms and reached for his hand, which he willingly gave to me. "It happened so fast," I told him as the crowd began to thin.

"I know," he said softly, and I could hear the relief that I was all right in his voice. We both knew how quickly that situation could have gotten dire. By the time I hit the floor, I was too low to feed myself anything, and no one else there knew what to do to help me. I looked to Jude, who stared back at me, completely pale and with a look of twisted panic and relief on his face.

I'd made a terrible mistake. I let my pride come before my health and it could have cost me my life. I should never had cared what people would have thought if I brought out my kit in the middle of a conversation or if I needed to ask for some food, and I knew better than to put off testing myself because it was an inconvenience. It had been a very long time since I'd experienced anything like that, and I knew the consequence was painful enough that it wasn't going to happen again.

"I want to go home," I said as I moved to get back on my feet. My hands were still shaking and I felt totally impaired. Nolan wrapped his arm around my waist to support me. I knew the next few hours would be an adventure, trying to regulate the highs and lows. Jude nodded to me and stepped out of our way.

"It's probably better you take her, Nolan. I don't know what to do if it happens again." Jude took another step away and grabbed my purse off the ground. He wasn't being a jerk; he was just scared, and I could understand that. I was scared too, and I would be safer with Nolan.

Jude handed me my purse and helped to brush some of the sugar off my face. "I'm sorry," he said. There was no doubt that he felt responsible for what had happened. I could see it on his face as he reached for my hand and held it for a second. "I'll call you tonight and see if you need anything."

"Thank you," I said, my voice shaky. "I'm sure I'll be fine."

"Give her a call later," Nolan said empathetically.

Erin, who had been standing with us, a look of bewilderment on her face, reached up and adjusted the collar on my shirt so that my bra wasn't showing. She offered a sympathetic smile. "Jude, can I get a ride home with you so Nolan can take her straight to her house?" she asked.

"Of course," he answered.

Nolan and I walked slowly down the aisle of the crowded dining room. People would try not to look as we walked by, but it was hard given that a few minutes ago I went down for the count in the middle of the packed room. I watched as parents tried to communicate to their kids not to stare and I wished they wouldn't make it such a big deal. Diabetes could be scary, but it wasn't something to make your children fearful of. "Almost out," he whispered next to me, and I knew he was seeing their eyes on us too.

He tucked me into his truck and buckled my seat belt. When we finally pulled out of the parking lot, every emotion that had been floating around my dizzy mind began to get clear and take root. I noticed my mouth was caked with sugar and spit. My lip was split and my head had a lump where I hit the floor when I couldn't stop myself. I was horrified and so deeply sad. Unable to hold back the tears any longer, I let them all go and sobbed the entire ride home. Nolan reached for my hand and held it tight as I rocked and shook with the force of my cries.

I was embarrassed that my classmates had seen me lose control of my body. I was disappointed that I ruined a date with Jude because I hadn't taken care of myself like I should've. I was scared that he wouldn't want to try again after what he'd seen tonight or maybe that he was such a nice guy I'd never know if he asked me out again because he felt like he had to out of pity for the way tonight had gone.

Nolan pulled into his driveway and parked the truck. He came around to my side and held his arms open to me, a look of empathetic heartbreak all over his face. He was hurting for me too. That had scared us both. I hesitated, worried I'd get him all messy with my current state, but he shook his head as if reading my thoughts and waved his hands toward himself, insisting I slide down and into his arms.

We stood in the driveway with him rocking me as he held me tight. I wanted the whole day to go away. I cried until there was nothing left. I cried until his entire shirt was wet with my tears and his lips had been pressed to my cheek a million times.

twenty-four

THE NEXT MORNING was rough. I opened my eyes and prayed I had dreamed the whole thing. Of course, I hadn't.

I spent my Sunday at home, lounging in bed and trying to recover from the embarrassment of the night before so I could go to school with my head held high on Monday. Nisha and Regan had begged me to go out to lunch with them, and when I'd refused, they brought lunch to me and had stayed long enough to watch a few episodes of a new serial show we'd been hearing about on Netflix. Nolan had been texting me all day, trying to get me to leave my house even if it just meant going over to his, but I had told him I was hanging out with the girls and that he should probably spend some time with Erin since he had to bail on their time together last night.

Before the girls went home, they asked me about my feelings for Jude. Nisha wanted to know, "Do you think about him all the time? I remember when Declan and I first got together, he was all I could think about."

Before I could even answer, Regan jabbed at her: "He's still all you can think about."

The three of us laughed, and Nisha didn't even try to deny it. I thought about Jude and how much I'd enjoyed the time we'd spent together. I liked him. We had a lot of the same interests and he made me laugh. I knew he was caring and genuine, which were important qualities for me. But I didn't think of him all the time. "Not really," I answered honestly. "I mean, I like him, but I don't think it's anywhere as intense as you and Declan."

Regan and Nisha traded glances quickly. Nisha asked, "Are you going to go out with him again?"

"I think so," I answered, but the way she'd asked the question had me wondering if maybe she thought that wasn't a good idea. "Why?"

"I'm not saying you have to be head over heels in love with the guy, but maybe he's not the right guy for you." She shrugged her shoulders and blew on her nails, which had a fresh coat of polish on them. "Let me ask you this—you have been single the entire time you've been in high school, so why all of a sudden have you decided you need to start dating?"

I gave her a soft kick with my foot, careful not to smudge my own freshly painted toenails. "Because you guys always made such a big deal out of it. And, I don't know, I guess I thought it was time to take that step."

"Well, you took it," Regan said. "Now you need to figure out if it was the right one or not. Jude is a great guy, but he isn't the only one out there."

"How do I know if he's the right one?" I asked.

"He'll give you butterflies in your stomach. He'll be the first person you think of when you wake up in the morning and the last you think of when you go to sleep. You want to be with him all the time and learn all the little details that make up his life. Nothing about him is boring." Nisha smiled as she listed the signs.

Regan nodded in agreement. "But," she added, holding up her finger and wet fingernail, "the real test is happiness." She sighed. "You know you're with the right person when you want them to be happy even if what it takes to make them happy makes you unhappy. And they would do the same for you. Sacrifice their own happiness for yours."

"Well, aren't you Miss Sunshine?" I asked sarcastically.

My brain felt like it was swimming around inside my head. How could I apply any of this to Jude? I guess only time would tell.

After Regan and Nisha left, my phone chimed with a text from Nolan.

TOP FIVE REASONS YOU NEED TO COME HANG OUT WITH ME.

I fought the smile that pulled at my lips. Another text came through.

1. Telling me you don't want to hang out is mean and hurts my feelings. You don't want to be mean, do you? Well, you are. . . .

I laughed out loud as the three dots appeared, chasing each other on my screen.

2. Many people in California are deficient in vitamin D. You must go outside in the sun to get it (right now you are locked up in your room like a hermit instead of soaking up the rays with me). Symptoms include explosive diarrhea, uncontrollable vomiting, beard growth in women, clucking like a chicken . . . ok I'm

making these up but don't you want to go down to the beach or something?

I didn't even have time to respond before another came through.

3. I want a Blaze Pizza from the mall but I can never remember where to park. If you make me go on my own there is a chance I'll go missing and it will be all your fault. You know I won't ask for directions. Don't be selfish.

He was dead serious. I had to give him step-by-step directions every time. It was as if his brain did not have the capacity to store the information necessary to learn the parking lot schematics of our local mall.

4. The models on my board are cold.

I was expecting another funny text so when the last one came through it made my heart feel too big for my chest.

5. I'm worried you're sitting in your room alone unhappy and it's killing me. If there is really nothing I can do to make you happy, then let me come over

and be unhappy with you. At least I won't have to imagine you're alone.

I told myself I'd text him back in an hour when I might be feeling up to doing something. I knew he'd push me to get back on my feet, and I was feeling petulant and wanted to procrastinate picking up my pieces a little longer. I grabbed a book and made myself comfy on my bed.

I could hear my parents downstairs making dinner as I sat on my bed, lost in the pages of my latest romance novel. As I turned the page, I heard my mom let out a little yelp and then the low timbre of my dad's laugh. Nolan was there. I couldn't hear what they were saying, but their voices rumbled from downstairs. When that quieted down, I knew he was headed up to my room. My door slowly opened and he peeked his head in.

"You're missing a beautiful day," he mentioned as he closed the door behind him and moved to sit in the chair at my desk. "Are you ever coming out of here again or will I need to start moving some of my clothes over so I can stay here and not miss you?" *That would be lovely,* I thought. Maybe I could just stay in here forever and not have to face anyone who saw me last night.

"Bring them over." I looked back to the page I was reading.

"What are you reading about?" I knew he really didn't

care and was just trying to make conversation.

"It's a romance." I held the cover up so he could see the hands clasped on the cover.

"That makes me a little sad." He made a pouty face.

"Me reading a romance makes you sad?"

"No, a romance book without a buff dude with his shirt hanging open and a woman clinging to his leg on the cover makes me sad. I thought that was a requirement. You know, half-dressed woman with bits and pieces almost falling out of her dress and a guy too interested in the horizon standing there with his foot propped up as she hangs from his body. Isn't that what you said should be on the cover?"

I laughed for the first time all day. "Maybe the ones at the library. Not the ones I have to bring to school." I tried to find my place on the page but was distracted when a Hershey Kiss was tossed and landed right on the page before sliding off and landing in my lap.

"I'm bored and you are being boring. Let's get out and do something." He stood up and slowly folded my book shut.

"I don't want to go anywhere."

"Staying inside won't change anything," he countered quickly.

"It will change that I have to face people today. Why do it today if I can put it off until tomorrow?"

"You have to just get back out there. People might be

curious about what happened, but if you hide away, it lets them fill in the blanks with their imagination and that is way worse." He reached for my ankles and clamped his hands around them.

"I don't want to see anyone yet. I'm just going to sit here and enjoy the evening in the comfort of my air-conditioning. Besides, I would hate to leave the poor characters of that book hanging just when they were getting to the good stuff."

"First of all"—Nolan narrowed his gaze on me—"you're not sitting." I was about to protest when he tugged my ankles quickly, sliding me down onto my bed. "Secondly, those characters can just put their throbbing, pulsing, hard, erect"—he paused a minute, as if he was trying to think of another descriptive word—"wet, and excitable body parts away for a little bit while you go enjoy real life with your friend." He left me lying on the bed as he retrieved my purple bikini from the top drawer. I crossed my arms and waited for him to explain the plan so I could shut it down.

"And third and finally, we aren't going somewhere you are going to see anyone, so there are no more excuses." He tossed my bikini onto my face.

"Where are we going, then?" I stood up, knowing that he was too persistent to try to fight off. I was leaving the house because if not, he was going to drag me down those stairs and shove me out the door. Nicely, but effectively nonetheless.

"We have"—he stopped long enough to look at his watch—"twenty minutes before the park sprinklers go on and I want to run through them with you."

"Waking up to the sprinklers trying to drown us the other day at the campout was not enough? You need to throw caution to the wind and jump right into another yard full of them?" I passed him and slipped inside my bathroom.

"It's on our list and we're running out of time." His words were muffled by the bathroom door. My heart missed a beat. I hated being reminded that one day he would no longer be my neighbor. "And I'm hoping the water will wash off your sad mood so I can have my friend back."

I tied the straps of the bikini top and slipped the bottoms up my legs, which luckily were already shaved thanks to the shorts I had to wear because of the heat. I shimmied a little to get them over my butt and then took my pump out of the pouch I had it in and clipped it like a pager to my bottoms. I grabbed a hair tie from the drawer and pulled my hair up into a messy bun.

"Fifteen minutes," Nolan sang outside the door. I rolled my eyes but laughed at the same time.

"You're very bossy, you know that?" I shouted through the door.

"I do know that."

I opened the bathroom door and stepped into my room,

tossing my clothes into my hamper near my closet. "I hope you're enjoying this. You're ruining my quiet evening reading." I walked up to stand right in front of him. He was sitting on the edge of my bed, reading out of the book I'd been reading when he walked in.

"This is really dirty," he whispered, giving me a wink. "I knew you read romances, but I imagined cowboys and corsets, not this."

"It's a great love story. I read it for that." I tried to take the book but he pulled it away gently.

"Sure it is." This time his wink was really big and exaggerated.

"Stop," I laughed, taking a firmer grip on my book and pulling it from his hands. He just laughed and stood up next to me.

"Let's go. I don't want to miss it. With all this drought talk they are only watering it twice a week."

I grabbed two towels out of the small closet outside my room. I tossed him one and we headed downstairs. My parents looked up as we entered the kitchen and I hated the relief that flitted across their faces seeing that I was actually leaving my room.

"We'll be back soon," I said as we opened the back door.

"Take your time. Dinner won't be ready for at least

another hour." My mom stopped cutting the vegetables and wiped her wet hands on a towel. "Nolan, I'd just like you to be aware that you'll be the one at fault if you scare me again while I have a knife in my hand. I can't help what happens." She smiled at him, but there was a spark of evil behind her eyes, and it made Nolan and me laugh.

We moved along the side of the house and out the front gate. I opened the towel and made it into a small cover-up for me as we walked down the block to the park at the end of our street. "So how do you know the sprinkler schedule?"

"I called the city. Told them I was concerned it wasn't being watered. They assured me—well, Mr. Walker, homeowner and concerned citizen—that they would have them on right at eight this evening and will let them run a bit longer to make sure the lawn gets adequate moisture."

"That was a lot of work." I shrugged and held tighter to the towel as a car drove past.

"Not really. Besides, it will be worth it when we are running through them. I was cooking up there in my room."

"No air-conditioning again, huh?" I laughed. His father thought that opening all the windows and turning on a few fans would cool the house down just as well as the air-conditioning would. Nolan hated it. He had tried proving to his dad numerous times that even with all the windows open and every fan they owned blasting at top speed, the house temperature barely dipped a degree. It didn't matter; his protests fell on deaf ears.

"I think the heat bakes his brain or something." He shook his head and looked defeated.

It was still a little light outside, but the sun was no longer visible in the sky. When we got to the park, Nolan set his towel down on a bench near the playground and waited for me to do the same. I looked around; there were still a few kids riding down the street on their bikes, or kicking a ball around on the grassy field. "Quit overthinking it and put your towel on the bench."

"Listen, Mr. McBossy. I hate just hanging out in my bikini. Sorry we can't all be as confident as you." I loosened up my hold a little. Nolan pulled his shirt off over his head and tossed it down into the pile he was creating. It made me happy to see that his shoulder was almost totally better. He'd been working on it at physical therapy every day during the week.

"Listen, Ms. I'm Beautiful but Refuse to Believe It, you are going to be freezing cold walking home dripping wet when we are done here if you don't have a dry towel." He kicked his flip-flops off under the bench and then put his hands on his hips, waiting for me to undress.

"Fine." I dropped my towel and tossed it onto his pile.

I then slipped off my sandals and pushed them under the bench with my feet. I decided my pump would be fine for the short time I'd planned on being in the water. I double-checked to make sure it was secure on my bottoms. The sprinklers weren't on yet so we had a little time. I headed for the swings and he followed. I sat down and he stood behind me, grabbing the chains so he could give me a push.

"Do you remember when I broke my wrist?"

"Yes," I answered harshly. "You scared the crap out of me!" I heard his deep laugh from behind me as he drew the swing back before releasing it.

"I was so sure I was going to land on my feet. I thought I was a cat or something. I didn't really account for the fact that the ground comes very quickly when you're flailing around after jumping from the highest point on a swing." He pushed me when I swung back. I kicked out my legs as I swung forward.

"I guess I should take some responsibility in it. I was the one who said you could do it." I laughed softly with a sigh. "I guess I've always thought you could do anything." I realized just how true that last sentence was. There was nothing he'd ever tried that he couldn't do. Jumping from a swing and landing on his feet being one of them, but it took a few more practices.

"That's why you're my best friend. It doesn't matter how crazy the idea was, you always had faith in me. It made—well, it makes me feel like a champion when I'm around you." He grabbed the chains and pulled me back even farther before letting me go again.

"I don't think your mom was very happy with me." I continued to kick out my legs and then pump them back as I gained some height.

"Don't be silly. She knows you could never talk me out of anything I get my heart set on. I think she was happy you were there to keep me from passing out on the way home. I swear I can still hear that awful snapping sound from when I tried to catch the full weight of my body with just one hand."

"I loved coming here with you." I looked out over the rest of the playground equipment and remembered all the hours we had spent pretending to be pirates or spacemen as we ran across the bridges and slid down every slide.

"Me too," he answered. "I'm going to miss it." Neither of us said anything for a few swings, my legs still working and his warm hand catching and then pushing my back. "Do you think we'll come back here one day with our kids?"

"Maybe."

It had only taken ten minutes for the sun to finish setting and the night to grow dark. The kids who had been playing outside disappeared into houses. In the stillness of the night air around us, the familiar hiss of sprinklers rang out. I jumped off the swing and the two of us took off out of the sand and onto the wet grass.

It was cold. So. Very. Cold. The water splashed across our chests and legs as we ran side by side through the spray. As we crossed the field, it seemed like we were going back in time. We left our eighteen-year-old minds behind and embraced the immature and playful minds of our younger years.

We laughed and giggled, pushed each other and fell as the cold water rained down on top of us. When the field became flooded, we took running starts, throwing ourselves down and sliding along the wet grass. I remembered being young and doing this so many years ago with Nolan. Memories flashed through my mind, each one brighter and louder than the last. The events of last night had no place in my thoughts when my consciousness was filled with such pure, unadulterated joy.

We were both on our backs, laughing loudly, when the sprinklers retreated and the park fell silent. My skin was cold, goose bumps covering every exposed inch. But even though I felt a physical chill all the way down to my bones, my heart and soul were very warm. Maybe running through sprinklers at the park is childish, but in the still of the night it became clear to me that there wasn't anything I could go through that laughter and Nolan couldn't wash away.

twenty-five

MONDAY MORNING I made my way up Nolan's stairs after saying good morning to his mom. I had given myself a small pep talk at home, assuring my reflection in the mirror in my bathroom it was possible to walk on campus with my head high no matter who had seen me at my worst. I knocked on Nolan's door as I pushed it open. As usual, he was still in the shower. I dropped my bag at the end of his bed and made my way over to his bulletin board to check on my girls. There was only one large poster up of a beautiful woman standing at the end of the stage in her bikini. Below the picture there was an article, which surprised me since he'd never hung anything like that up before.

She was absolutely stunning. A tall, smiling woman, proudly showing off her amazing body. I put my hand on the handle of the drawer in his desk, about to retrieve the paper I would need to cover her up, when I saw something in the picture that made me do a double take. I leaned in closer, certain I was mistaken. My breath caught in my throat and I felt my eyes sting with tears.

That gorgeous woman who was hanging proudly from my best friend's bulletin board had an insulin pump clipped to her bikini bottoms. If you didn't look closely you'd almost miss it against the dark fabric of her bottoms. The closer I looked, the clearer it became that this woman had not been ashamed at all of her pump, but instead wore it proudly for everyone to see.

I could tell from the picture she was young and in some sort of competition. My gaze dropped down to the text where I read that her name was Sierra Sandison and she was a twenty-year-old beauty contestant in the Miss America pageant. She hadn't been trying to make a big deal out of her diabetes, but simply clipped her pump to her bikini and took the stage. What she hadn't realized she was doing was showing the world and all the other little girls who wore their own pumps that it didn't take away from their beauty.

I continued to read about her, completely in awe of this

inspiring woman. Little girls across the country had been searching for her picture, so she had posted it to social media and it caught fire. Miss Idaho was a type 1 diabetic and she had just helped heal a little part of my heart that had been hurt with the thoughts of returning to school and facing everyone who had seen me fall. I wiped a tear from my cheek and tried to pull it together. I knew I'd never cover her. She could stay right there in all her inspiring beauty. She was perfect just the way she was.

"I was hoping you wouldn't cover her." His voice was quiet behind me. I hadn't even heard him step out of the bathroom. I'd been too wrapped up in reading her story. I turned around to look at him as he leaned against the door frame of his bathroom.

"I can't believe I've never heard her story. She's so pretty." I looked back over my shoulder again.

"I told you a pump doesn't make you any less beautiful. I hope seeing her will make you finally believe it." He pushed off the door frame and headed for his dresser. He was already dressed in shorts and a T-shirt as he retrieved a pair of socks.

"Thank you." The words didn't quite feel like enough, but I knew he understood what I couldn't say.

I couldn't stop myself from closing the distance between us and throwing myself into his arms. He caught me and laughed as he wrapped his arms around my waist to keep me from falling. I closed my eyes and held him tightly. When I finally pulled my face from the crook of his neck, I planted a kiss right on his forehead. "Thank you," I said just before I kissed his head again.

"I knew it," Seth said from the doorway, and I looked over my shoulder at him while Nolan leaned to the side to see past my body as he held me.

"You don't know anything," Nolan joked. He loosened his arms and I slid down his body.

"So you're leaving me for him, huh?" Seth continued. "I thought we were good together." I walked over to him and messed up his hair.

"It will always be you, love," I teased, kissing him softly on his cheek.

"All right. Enough." Nolan sighed, smiling at both of us as he retrieved his socks, which had fallen to the floor when I jumped in his arms. "What do you want?"

"Mom told me to let you know the physical therapist's office called and needed to move your appointment to five tonight."

"Thanks," Nolan replied, tucking his feet into his shoes.

"No problem." Seth blew me a kiss and then shut the door. Nolan rolled his eyes, but I could see the corners of his lips fighting a smile.

■ ■ ■

I thought I would be a lot more nervous walking into school than I actually ended up feeling. Nolan was trying hard to keep me distracted, telling me about all the differences he'd found so far between *The Walking Dead* comics and the TV show on AMC. He liked to make predictions about what was going to happen next on the show based on what had happened in the graphic novels. His technique worked, and by the time we got to my locker, it felt like any other Monday at school.

After gathering everything I needed from mine, we headed over to his. The school was decorated with posters announcing the dates for prom. Nolan and I had gone to many school dances together, but he would almost definitely go with Erin this year. As for me, I wasn't sure who my date would be. Maybe Jude and I would go together or maybe I'd just go with some friends.

Nolan stopped at the door of my classroom and pulled me aside. "You walk with your head up high today or I'm going to hold you down and tickle you until you scream." He tapped my nose and made me smile. He reached into his pocket and handed me some candy Kisses. "Just in case you need a pick-me-up." Kids pushed past us and stepped into classes while others acted like they had all the time in the world to sit around and chat with friends. "Start thinking about that road trip, okay?" Nolan took a step back. "Let's cross it off our list during spring break."

"Sounds good," I agreed even though I didn't know if my parents would be okay with me going anywhere alone for a few nights. I was old enough that they couldn't really stop me, but I'd never go without their blessing. I also wasn't sure that Nolan had thought about Erin and how she'd feel about us going away on a trip together.

"Head up, Sugar," he said one last time before turning and heading to his class. I knew right then that I'd be spending the entire day dreaming about escaping this town for the wide-open road with him. It really didn't matter where we went—I only cared about being where he was.

twenty-six

"SO WHAT EXACTLY is your assignment?" I asked my friend Sasha as we left the school newspaper meeting the following Monday. I was really excited because I'd been assigned to interview students about the mandatory pep rallies our school held after one group of students began protesting them last month. It was going to be a great story, and Sasha had even offered to introduce me to her cousin who had organized the rally resistance. She'd also asked if she could talk to some of my friends at lunch.

"I'm writing about the remarkable things that happened to us this year. I feel like there is so much negative news going on in the world, I just want to write something that makes people smile. I want it to be happiness in print. I want students to connect with other students through shared joy." Sasha was practically beaming. I still had no idea what she was writing about, but I always loved her work when she was finished.

"Okay, then let's get you started." I led her out to where Nisha, Regan, Declan, and Nolan were sitting. I'd also let Jude know we'd be there if he'd wanted to join us. Once again the smell of burgers on the barbecue had called to Declan like a siren would a pirate.

I sat across from Nolan with Jude and Sasha, leaving the open space next to him for Erin, who was almost to our group, her lunch in hand. I gave her a smile and a wave when she took her seat at his side. "Hi, everyone," I said now that the group was all there. "This is Sasha and she writes for the paper with me. She needs to ask everyone some questions and I told her you would help her out because I need her to help me out. So please be cool."

Everyone laughed and agreed to help. Sasha slipped her backpack off her shoulders and pulled out her notebook. "Okay. I'm doing a piece on remarkable moments. I just want your honest response. I can also leave your name off if you want to be anonymous, but I'm hoping you don't because it's much more fun for our readers if they know who you are."

"Scandalous," Declan teased.

"I'll ask the question and we'll just go around the circle answering it. I think that's the easiest way," Sasha said, squinting her eyes as she counted our group members. "I won't need your answers, Mackenzie."

"Sweet," I replied as I pulled out my kit and tested myself.

"Okay, first question. What was the most remarkable win you had this year? It can be social, educational, sports . . ." Sasha let her voice trail off.

To answer in an orderly direction, Jude went first. "I won a regional surfing competition."

Declan went next. "I was accepted into Arizona State."

"I was accepted at NYU," Nisha said next. Her smile faltered and Declan reached for her hand.

Regan answered easily. "I asked my crush out and she said yes."

Erin was already smiling. She turned and looked at Nolan. "I started dating my crush too."

I was glad I didn't have to share anything because in that moment it felt like my brain was wiped of all epic moments. Nolan's eyes met mine and he paused in thought. I looked down at my lunch.

"I didn't reinjure my shoulder," he answered. I looked up and saw Erin lean her head on it. I pulled my sandwich from my lunch bag, wondering if maybe I shouldn't have offered up my friends so easily.

"Great," Sasha cooed. "Tell me about your most remarkable kiss this year."

I told myself not to look up at Nolan, but the message came too late. Our eyes locked for a brief second before we both looked away. I could feel the sharp pain where I'd drawn my bottom lip between my teeth and the heat that had risen to my cheeks.

Jude smiled when I looked at him. "After Italian food with a girl who hates bachelor groupies almost as much as she loves zombies."

Nisha, Regan, and Erin all said, "Aww," and I knew I should have been swooning, but I was feeling anxious instead. Jude deserved better than that. The guilt from what Nolan and I had done was back and I could hardly stand to be sitting there with Erin as if it had never happened. I tried to smile and I think I pulled it off, but I refused to look at anyone and I could see out of the corner of my eye that Nisha and Regan had their eyes on me, as if they could sense that something wasn't right.

I slipped my backpack off my shoulders and tugged off my sweatshirt. When did it get so hot? Heat spread up my neck and across my chest. Declan was oblivious to my freak-out and answered the question with the typical swagger he lived his whole life with. "Every time I kiss Nisha it's remarkable. But I think the best kiss this year was at homecoming under those little twinkling light things. What are those called?"

Silence met his question.

"Babe?" he asked. "Nisha!"

"What?" She finally turned to him.

"What were those little twinkling lights called that you liked at the homecoming dance? You know, the ones you made us take ten thousand selfies with?"

Nisha shook her head a few times, and I looked at Regan, who had never taken her eyes off me. She skillfully raised one brow. She was onto me. My only saving grace was that they were probably both assuming I was flustered by Jude talking about our first kiss. They wouldn't assume it had been the memory of Nolan kissing me that had turned my world upside down again.

"I don't know," Nisha answered. She looked at me, her expression confused and pleading all at once. She knew something was up. God, now I couldn't breathe! Was my throat getting smaller? I put my hand around it just to check.

"What about your most remarkable kiss?" Sasha asked

Nisha, trying to stay on track and equally as oblivious as Declan.

"Homecoming," Nisha said succinctly.

Regan was up next, and she squinted her eyes and answered, "I kissed my crush and it was epic." I thought we were going to move on, but then Regan added pointedly, "But . . . my friends already knew that because I. Don't. Keep. Secrets. From. Them."

Dammit.

Erin looked to Regan and then back to me. Clearly there was some friend drama happening, but she didn't know the half of it. No one did. Well, no one but the boyfriend at her side and me. She shook it off and smiled as she answered Sasha's prompt. "My most remarkable kiss this year was at the beach bonfire. There is something about the waves and the glow of the fire that makes it so romantic, right?"

Thank God it was almost over. Nolan just had to share his most remarkable kiss and we could move on. I could stuff this day away in my memory and then block it out like I had the memory of the night in the Jacuzzi with Nolan. I held my breath as he took forever to respond. Every eye in the group was on him, every ear ready to hear the story of his most remarkable kiss.

He looked at Erin, and even though she was smiling up at him, his lips were not curling for her the way they should be and my lungs ceased their movement. His head turned in my direction and I pleaded with him silently to do the right thing for his relationship. He did not need to lie to save our friendship, and I had already begun to mend my own feelings so the responsibility to save them did not rest on his shoulders.

He drew in a deep breath and I knew before he even began that he was about to make a huge mistake, and one that would not be easy to repair.

"Mine was unexpected," Nolan said, his eyes on mine, leaving no doubt that he was talking to me and possibly leaving little doubt to our close friends that he was talking about me.

"Don't," I begged softly. I shook my head. "You didn't have to do that. You know it meant nothing." I grabbed my stuff as fast as I could as our friends sat in shocked silence. Just before I pushed up to my feet, I looked Erin in the eye. "I'm so sorry."

Once I was on my feet, I offered my hand to Jude. "Can I help you up? I'd like to walk you to your next class. I think we have a few things to talk about."

He only hesitated long enough to throw a glance in Nolan's direction. I'm not sure if he was afraid Nolan was going to challenge him somehow or if he wasn't sure he wanted to get in the middle of all the drama he'd found himself in. In the end, he gave me a tight smile and put his hand in mine.

I wasn't sure what I was going to say, but I knew it was time to be honest with myself and with him about my feelings. "I'm sorry about the way that just happened. The kiss between Nolan and me was before you and I went out on our first date."

"I knew he liked you," he said, nudging me with his shoulder.

"No, it's actually the other way around. I'm sorry." I made myself look up at his face even though I was ashamed for letting him find out about the kiss in such a terrible way and for not being honest with him about my feelings for Nolan when he'd asked about our relationship at the bonfire.

"It sucks, but I'm not mad at you," he said. "Obviously I know what it's like to be into someone more than they're into you. But if you want my opinion," he said, and I looked up at him because I did want to hear what he was thinking, "Nolan is totally into you. The guy just completely destroyed his relationship for you." He winced as he said it. "That was brutal out there."

I shook my head. "He thought his choice was his relationship with her or his friendship with me. We would always choose our friendship over anything else."

The bell rang, letting us know that lunchtime was over.

Jude stopped us outside his class. "The way you describe your relationship with him, it sounds like your friendship is never really at risk, Mackenzie. Maybe Nolan was really choosing you this time."

Nolan was waiting for me by his truck after school. I'd had the conversation I wanted to have with him a hundred times in my head in fifth and sixth period, but when we were alone in the cab of his truck, I had no idea what to say to him. He spoke first as he drove us home.

"I'm sorry, Zie. Were you able to fix things with Jude?"

"He understood what happened between us. It wasn't the best way to find out, but it was a conversation that was overdue. What about you? Was Erin hurt? Were you able to explain that it meant nothing to us? It was just a silly lesson." I thought about the look on her face when I'd apologized. The way she'd had tears in her eyes and had let her hands fall to her lap instead of tangling them around Nolan.

Nolan was quiet for a long moment, as if he was struggling with whether or not to tell me everything. Finally he said, "She was hurt, of course. I was honest with her like I should have been the night it happened."

"Maybe she just needs time," I said, trying to be hopeful that he didn't just throw away his relationship for nothing.

"Time isn't going to fix this problem."

"I'm sorry," I told him as we pulled into his driveway. "I wish that kiss had never happened."

Nolan's hand froze on his handle, his eyes closed. "I'm sorry too, Zie."

twenty-seven

NOLAN GAVE THE parking attendant a small wave as we passed through the orange cone maze they had set out through the entire parking structure. We hadn't thought that Disneyland would be crowded on a Wednesday, but it looked like they were expecting tons of people. We went around another curve and then were led out to a large ramp where we'd have to ascend to the top level and park. Car after car slid into the spots they were directed to like a perfectly timed synchronized swimming routine. We were barely able to get our doors open before the cars on either side opened, spilling tons of kids into the space around us.

Last night as I was lying awake in my bed unable to sleep, Nolan had sent me a text letting me know that his coach had a family emergency and practice had been canceled. It was something that never happened so he wanted to take advantage of his free afternoon and cross another item off our list. The timing couldn't have been more perfect. We needed to escape the drama our secret had caused and have some fun reminding ourselves why we were willing to risk everything to keep our friendship.

Nolan was carrying a backpack that contained our sweatshirts, sunscreen, and of course my kit. My mom had bought the tickets for us after checking with Mrs. Walker and then calling the school to get our work for the day. If you live anywhere near the park, you know that the best days to go to Disneyland are the midweek days of any season that isn't summer or Halloween or Christmas. If you don't follow those guidelines, you will spend hundreds of dollars to wait in lines for hours to ride two rides and get a sunburn and tired feet. That's how we found ourselves riding the large escalator down to the trams at nine in the morning on a school day.

We climbed onto the tram and rode it up to the front gates. The last time we'd been there together was two years ago, but our families had been with us. It felt completely different scanning our tickets and stepping onto Main Street just the two of us. We skipped getting a locker since we had only brought the necessities, far less stuff than when our moms had packed for the day. I knew he had slipped some snacks inside our sweatshirts just in case I dropped low and we weren't anywhere close to food.

We'd stayed up late texting ideas for the day. We both agreed the best plan was to head to Space Mountain for our first ride of the day since it was our favorite. After that we'd head over to the Matterhorn. Everything went as planned, and we were standing in the line only ten minutes after entering the front gates.

"Have you given any thought to where you want to go for spring break?" Nolan nudged me forward in line when I'd gotten distracted by a cute little girl twirling on the ropes while waiting with her family.

"Where are the boundaries?" I asked. I didn't know if he was thinking of a quick drive up the coast and then back down or if he was trying to cross a state line.

"I talked to my mom about it a little yesterday and she said as long as we keep our phones on and promise to check in, she didn't mind if we stayed somewhere for a night or two. I guess that gives us a pretty good range."

We took another few steps up in line as I thought of all the possibilities. "I'd like to see the London Bridge in Arizona." We'd driven through the state on our way to Texas one year, but we never got to stop and see the famous bridge. There was something about its beauty and age that appealed to me.

"You never got over that, did you?" he asked referring to the fact that I'd really had a fit when I learned we wouldn't be stopping there. Nolan had the aliens in New Mexico and I wanted the bridge in Arizona. We simply did not have the time over our vacation to see everything.

"No," I answered simply.

"Sounds fine to me. I could use a little sun and lake time." We descended a ramp to the front of the line and held up two fingers to indicate the number of riders in our party.

"Row one, please," the cast member said, waving us along to the front of the cart. My smile was so wide it made my cheeks numb. I loved that ride more than any other I'd ever been on. Riding a roller coaster in the dark made it so much more thrilling than any other where you could see the tracks in front of you.

We climbed in side by side and Nolan set the backpack down between his feet on the floor. I lowered the bar that would serve as a seat belt during the ride and pulled up on it to show the cast member that I was in snug.

Once all the riders were in, the cart moved forward toward the control room and we turned into a dark tunnel that was quickly lit up by lights streaming past like stars.

"I hope this never changes," Nolan said as the force of our movement pushed us back against our seats.

I turned my head to watch him and found that he was looking at me. "The ride?" I asked loudly, the soundtrack loud in the small tunnel. He just shook his head a little, but the ride sent us up the tracks and out onto the top of the roller coaster. It took a few twists to adjust to the jerking motion and the way my stomach felt pushed to the bottom of my gut as we raced around the turns. By the time we flew over a few small bumps and zoomed around another set of curves in the opposite direction, I was smiling and screaming, holding my hands high above my head.

At the end of the ride, we were shot into a tunnel where the stars zip past you again and a picture is snapped. Loud sounds of air brakes echoed through the large building as the cart was delivered back to the front of the line. We jumped out and headed to the exit. The ground below us reminded me of bubble wrap as it dropped us into the gift shop and past the screens where our pictures were displayed. We didn't stop to see them since our Fastpasses that we'd managed to grab on our way in only had five minutes left before they expired.

I decided to wait until we weren't around so many people to ask Nolan what he meant about things changing. A million thoughts were racing through my mind as we dipped under the ropes and zigzagged through the line designated for Fastpass holders. The second time was just as thrilling as the first, and soon we found ourselves staring at a picture of us smiling with our eyes wide open. It was good for a laugh but we definitely weren't bringing it home for anyone else to see.

Together we walked out of the dark passageway next to the arcade and Pizza Port. We headed straight to the next ride, opting to wait in line on the side of the Matterhorn that was known to go faster than the other. The bobsleds were different than they had been the last time we were there. You used to have to sit in a line with someone between the other person's legs, but now every rider got their own seat. It was also a little scarier inside, but I'm not sure if that was because it was actually scarier due to the renovation or if my fear of the monster inside the mountain had just grown and multiplied until every little growl made me jump.

When we got off that ride, I knew my blood sugar was crashing. "I need something to eat," I said as I pointed to a churro stand just outside the exit. With churros in hand and a big bottle of cold water, we found a small curb beneath the monorail track that was shaded and sat down to enjoy our treats. I checked myself and discovered I was only sixty so I ate the churro and only gave myself a small bolus of insulin. We watched as families walked past us with children dressed in various costumes. There seemed to be princesses everywhere I looked.

After chewing enough to start feeling a little better, I decided to ask Nolan about his question. "What did you mean in there?" I asked, gesturing to Space Mountain.

He chewed his bite and took a swig of water. He shrugged his shoulder a little. "I guess I meant, I hope we have another fifty years of celebrating our friendship. I hope we never stop making lists and hanging out. I hope we never let not being neighbors anymore come between us." He wiped his mouth with the back of his hand. "I feel like this couldn't have happened by accident." He motioned with his hand between the two of us. "We get along too well for it to be a random act of the universe."

"Are you saying we were friend soul mates?" I bumped his shoulder with mine and took another bite, cinnamon falling all over my shirt.

"If that's a thing, then yes." He moved the wrapping from his churro down so he could get a bigger bite. "I'm realizing now what you and I are might one day be limited because we're growing up." He took his bite.

"What do you mean?" I swooped in and took a bite of his churro while he was thinking.

"We're not going to work at the same place, so I won't get to see you in the morning or give you a ride home. And maybe we won't even get to eat lunch together if our companies aren't close. If we take jobs in different cities or different states, our interaction with each other might be through the screens of our computers instead of face-to-face on the counter of your parents' kitchen." He spelled out some of the fears I'd also had when I thought of our future, and then he removed the wrapper from his churro completely and pushed the rest of it into his mouth. I laughed because it was way too big of a bite but he wasn't going to give up.

"We'll just have to make it work. I'd be willing to make choices that kept me close to where you are." I tried to act normal, like I hadn't just confessed to possibly shaping my life around his. I moved to retrieve my sunglasses from the backpack and handed him his too. He nodded and tried hard to shove the sweet dough between his lips with his finger. He brushed off his hands and stood up from the curb, reaching down to help me up as I finished my own churro. We tossed the wrappers into the trash and started heading toward Big Thunder Mountain.

"I'd do the same," he said, matching my casual tone.

I kept my eyes focused on the walkway in front of us. We reached the line and began to wind along the big rocks and down to the small pond of copper-colored water. We stopped as the line appeared in front of us. I let his words sink in, feeling my shoulders relax with the reassurance that we would both be fighting to keep our friendship in the months that were coming. Summer might be days of hanging out at each other's houses and family trips together, but by fall there would be way more space between us than a few hedges and an old fence. Behind us an old train circled the big mountain and careened down the rickety track, splashing water as it made its final drop.

We took a few steps up and were met again by a cast member, who asked us to stand in row four. "Are you secure?" the cast member asked as she pulled up on the metal bar.

"Yes," Nolan and I answered together, giving each other a reassuring smile as the bar fell back heavily to our laps.

"Then you're ready. Enjoy the ride."

twenty-eight

WE CAME HOME from Disneyland drenched from the rain and exhausted. Clouds had filled the sky three hours before the park closed, but didn't burst until just before they shut it down. Families started packing up when the whole sky was covered with rain clouds and most of the rides we could just walk right on. It was an amazing way to experience the theme park.

We suffered the consequences the next day when we had to drag ourselves out of bed for school after only a few hours of sleep. It didn't matter; I wouldn't have traded any of it for all the money in the world. We had reexperienced something from our childhood together, and another item had been crossed off our napkin list. Now only the two big items remained—tattoos and a road trip.

Spring break was just a week away. I told my parents about our plans to go on a road trip, and while they didn't immediately shoot it down, they didn't give me permission right away either. They were worried that we might not be safe driving across the desert alone and wanted time to talk to the Walkers about it. We might be adults, but we still lived under their roofs, and had to go along with whatever they decided. I pretended like I'd be okay with whatever they said, but deep down the truth was I'd be devastated if they forbade us from going.

Nolan and I were back in sixth period when my phone vibrated in my pocket. I pulled it out and saw that, once again, it was a message from him while sitting next to me. I smiled and shook my head at him.

NOLAN: Game night. I get to bet you $5 our moms are drunk before 9 this time.

ME: It's only fair.

NOLAN: I hope they get drunk before talking about our road trip.

ME: Have your parents said anything more about it?

NOLAN: They told me they were going to let your

parents make the decision.

ME: I don't know how to sway them in our favor.

NOLAN: Pot brownies?

ME: Ha! Yeah just let me call up my dealer.

NOLAN: Pay them off. I have $546. What are you bringing to the table?

ME: I have been saving my allowance and report card money all year . . . $450.

NOLAN: I don't think that will do the trick.

ME: Tie them up? Blackmail?

NOLAN: I guess we have to use the last resort tool. Guilt.

ME: On it.

I started that afternoon with my mom. We were folding some laundry on the couch before my dad got home from work. "I was thinking about how much I'm going to miss this," I said as I folded a sweater and placed it in my pile.

"Folding laundry?"

"No, spending time with you. Once I get busy with college and studying, there isn't going to be as much time for friends and family." BINGO. My mom held a shirt of mine close to her and froze. I could tell she hadn't really thought about me managing my time while in college. Maybe she just assumed it would be like high school since I was staying close to home. The reality was that I'd have to divide up my diminished free time between studying, family, and friends.

"I'm sure you'll find time to work everyone in," she said, recovering, finishing the fold and laying it in my pile.

"I'm sure," I said softly, "there will just have to be sacrifices." I reached for a towel and held it out. "I'll come home and see you and Dad a lot, but my friends will be away at their schools. I think Nolan and I will have to see a lot less of each other. He will have a different schedule and we might not even get to see each other at all during the week. Then there will be his baseball schedule too." The words easily flowed from my mouth because I'd been thinking about the logistics of our friendship and how exactly it might change at the end of summer. It was all so heartbreaking.

"He will be very busy," my mom said as she reached for a pair of yoga pants. "You guys still have the whole summer to hang out, though. Maybe you'll be sick of each other by then." She smiled a very motherly smile that was meant to be reassuring. She could have promised me a year more of hanging out with Nolan like we always had and it would have never been enough. When it came to him, I would always want more.

"You're so right." My mom always liked to think she was able to share knowledge with me and answer all of my questions. It's like the time she'd told me I'd understand where babies came from one day after Regan had already spilled the beans in fourth grade. "I think we both want to make the best of this summer, you know, with it being our last before we have to grow up."

I saw my mom's fluid movement folding the clothes become rigid again. I hoped I hadn't taken it too far and made her sad. I'd heard tons of horror stories of moms falling to pieces when their children "left the nest." I could always remind her I'd still be staying close to her nest if the tears came. I watched her face carefully and was relieved when she fluttered her eyes but didn't cry.

"Whatever you guys decide about the trip we'll totally understand. I mean, there are plenty of times as adults that we'll be able to get away together. I'm sure we can get vacation time at our jobs and miss some time in college. Then of course our families will understand." I knew my mom liked to think of me as young and innocent, untouched by the hard realities of life. But even I was surprised when she fell for that. Nolan was already going to miss class for games and I would need to save my missed days for when I wanted to cover stories happening during times I was scheduled to be in class. Taking time off from new jobs would also be difficult.

"Sure, honey," she said. I knew I had her. When we

finished folding the clothes, I gave her a big hug and headed up to my room.

ME: Got her.

NOLAN: Well done. Fingers crossed. T minus two hours. Avengers?

ME: Thank you and no way.

NOLAN: Is it going to be a no until I pick a Channing movie?

ME: Of course not. Don't be silly. G.I. Joe?

NOLAN: Sure!

Two minutes passed while I waited for him to discover my trick. I pulled out my math book and grabbed my pencil.

NOLAN: Dirty trick.

ME: You say dirty trick, I say win-win.

NOLAN: See you later (imagine that said in the most begrudging tone).

ME: Looking forward to it (imagine that as patronizing as possible).

I finished my homework right before I heard the back door open and the Walkers greeting my parents. The sound of someone on the stairs made me smile. I was already so invested in this trip I knew tonight would either be an epic victory or an epic disappointment. When Nolan opened the door, he was smiling ear to ear. "What'd you do?" I asked, knowing that he was giddy for a reason.

"Nothing," he said, sounding bored. "I was just telling your mom how much I was going to miss running over here to see you." He jumped onto my bed and climbed up to my pillows. "You know, with all the studying and baseball we will hardly get to hang out. It's such a shame, really." He couldn't help the laugh that slipped out. He held his hand up and I rolled my eyes but gave him a high five. Any guilt added to what my mom was already feeling would only help our case.

"Well, bless our hearts," I said sadly; then I held my hand out and waited for my chocolate treat. He brought his hand up to his chest and rested it over his heart. "Okay, it's blessed enough." I laughed and he feigned offense before reaching into his pocket and putting the three shiny treasures in the palm of my hand.

"You're going to miss that," he said seriously, pointing to the Kisses in my hand.

"I am." I could have joked or teased him about the sentimental tone he had used, but the reality was there was no denying it. I was truly going to miss it. Miss the way he was so attentive, the way he knew me, and of course the way he took care of me sometimes without making me feel like a child. I popped a Kiss into my mouth and chewed it slowly. "You're going to miss my bad moods," I said around the chocolate. I was expecting a smart-ass response, but he just looked at me and nodded.

"I am." It happened again in that moment. My brain made the words *I love you* easily available at the tip of my tongue so I could tell him how I felt. Instead, I chewed my chocolate, and when it was finished, I put another one in my mouth.

He watched me with a tender look as I finished the treat and then he opened his arms so I could crawl in beside him. He had already ordered our movie on my Amazon Prime account and by the time I was comfy, the movie started. It wasn't even an hour later that our moms were cracking up in the kitchen and we knew that our fate had been decided—just not which way the vote had gone.

twenty-nine

IT WAS TOTALLY happening. My mom and dad agreed to let me go with Nolan to Lake Havasu to see the London Bridge. It was the farthest I had ever been away from them and Mom was being a little neurotic, worrying about all the bad things that could possibly happen to me on the road. I listened to every piece of advice, and every little time she thought of something new I should try to remember. I knew that it would be hard for any parent to let their kid leave the state alone for the first time, but for my parents there was an extra level of planning that had to go into it.

Crossing the state line meant I'd be out of the care of my

endocrinologist. I would need to bring anything I'd need along with me because it would not be like I could just have my doctor call in something I'd forgotten since he would not be a doctor practicing in that state. My relationship and history with my doctors was built over time. Other kids might need stitches if they were out of town and any doctor or hospital would do. Being diabetic meant that my options when sick in another state would be limited, especially if it was the weekend.

Not all doctors knew the nuances of the disease, and they certainly didn't have a detailed history of my highs and lows like my doctor at home had in my chart. Many of my supplies and medications needed approval through my insurance company, which was a long process that involved multiple steps and ended in them being mailed to my home in bulk. It wasn't like I could just walk into a pharmacy and walk out with a few days' worth.

Friday night I packed my bags and watched as my mom fussed about how much of each medical supply I would need. The plan was to leave early Saturday morning and stay there for the weekend, returning home on Monday. We had two nights of freedom roughly five hours away from home. I made sure to pack for the hot weather and for the time we'd be spending at the lake.

Choosing where to stay had been a little difficult. We'd

never been there, so picturing where exactly each place was in relation to the bridge was difficult, but thankfully the internet helped narrow everything down. My mother had found a condo on the lake that could be rented for a few days at a time and the pictures showed the bridge in the background. It was perfect.

Mr. and Mrs. Walker booked it under their name since we weren't so sure how the owners would feel about teens renting their beautiful vacation home. They lived in Phoenix and wouldn't be around at all, so the key was to be left in a lock box and we were to use a code to open it. Nolan and I offered to pay for the rental, but our parents split it, calling the whole thing our graduation gifts. Some other seniors from school were going on a senior trip to Mexico the same week, and I think our parents were just grateful that was of no interest to us. I never did see the fun in naked bungee jumping.

I was so excited Friday night after we packed up the car that I could barely sleep. I thought of how great it was going to be to have two full days of time with Nolan, and of course the long drive there made it feel like we were finally adults, able to take care of ourselves. While I was thrilled our plan had been given the green light, a part of me was also sad that going on this trip would only leave one thing on the napkin list. I wasn't ready then, but maybe the trip would help get me there.

I was up an hour before my alarm was going to wake me. I took a shower and put on a comfy outfit for the ride. I tested myself and ate my breakfast while I waited for Nolan to come get me. My mom was trying not to hover over me in the kitchen, but I could tell the whole trip was really causing her a lot of stress.

"I promise I'll be okay," I assured her as she sat down with her coffee at the kitchen table. I took another bite of my bagel and cream cheese.

"I'm sure you'll be fine. If anything happens, Nolan knows how to take care of you." She smiled, but it fell quickly and she tried to cover it by taking another sip of her coffee.

"I'm not going to be that far away. I'll call you every day." I reached out and put my hand on top of hers. She just nodded.

Sitting across from my mom at that table, I really looked at her. I saw the years of worry in the small lines by her eyes and the dark circles from years of never being able to sleep completely peacefully. I appreciated her so much it felt like the emotion would spill right out of me. Instead, I leaned forward and kissed her cheek before wrapping my arms around her and pulling us together for a tight hug.

"I love you, Mom."

"I love you too."

The kitchen door opened and Nolan stepped inside. He

put his hands up in surrender. "No knife today?" He stepped cautiously past her and over to the counter where the bagels were kept.

"Not yet," she answered with a smile.

"My brothers wiped out all of our breakfast foods so unless I wanted mac and cheese for breakfast, I have to steal a bagel." He twirled open the bag and grabbed a plain bagel from inside.

"Help yourself," my mom said as she stood up. "I'm going to go get dressed so I can embarrass you by running after your truck when you guys leave." She said it so seriously that I was afraid to laugh in case she meant it. She squeezed my shoulder as she walked by, and Nolan grabbed the cream cheese from the fridge and moved to sit down next to me.

"Are you almost ready?" he asked before taking a big bite.

"Just finished my breakfast. I'm ready when you are." I crumpled up the paper towel I'd had my breakfast on and tossed it in the trash.

"I looked up our options for how to get there and I think we should make it there in about five hours if we follow most of the traffic laws." He pulled a piece of paper out of his back pocket and set it on the table. I unfolded it and found a printout of the route he'd picked. I loved the way our path twisted and turned like an uncoordinated snake out of town and into the California desert before crossing the state line over the thin blue squiggly line that represented the Colorado River.

"Are we going to stop anywhere?" I asked him as he chewed his breakfast. I reached up and wiped a dab of cream cheese off his lip and wiped it on his paper towel.

"Probably stop for lunch if we get hungry. I thought we could drive until something looked good. Just bring a few snacks in case there is a long stretch without food and you get low." I stood up and grabbed a grocery bag, stuffing it full of my favorite snacks as he finished eating.

"Well," he said with a big smile as he stood up and tossed the paper towel in the trash. "I guess it's time." My stomach flipped and then fluttered as my heart pounded in my chest. I was so excited for the trip and might have let out a small squeal. Nolan chuckled and grabbed the snack bag from my hand. "Go tell your parents good-bye. If your mom was serious about chasing down the truck, let her know to get her shoes on."

My mom had been kidding, of course, but all of our parents did stand at the end of the driveway after delaying our trip a half hour reminding us to call and then giving tips and a year's worth of car knowledge in two minutes. Nolan's dad was the greatest offender in that area, showing us twice how to check the oil even though Nolan had been changing his own oil for two years.

When we finally turned at the end of our block, our parents no longer visible in the rearview mirror, we both laughed. I'm not sure if it was from the relief of the stress we were feeling radiating off the adults or if it was because we felt like we had gotten away with something. It didn't matter, really; we laughed because we loved to laugh and because we were about to cross the state line on a road trip that had to be epic simply because it would be our first and most likely our last alone together.

We listened to music for the first two hours of the drive. I had my feet up on the dashboard by the time we hit what appeared to be the first expanse of desert. It was weird to me how the city gave way to open land, and the houses that were literally built on the edge of the freeway seemed to run toward the large, rocky mountains as we crossed city lines. Small cars filled with families running weekend errands grew less and less frequent, while large Mack trucks grew in number, sharing the highway with us. I tried to look at everything. I wanted to remember it all, but I found myself watching him a lot too.

"Are you hungry?" he asked, turning down the music, which was more static than tune at that point.

"Yes. I probably should eat." I sat up in my seat and slipped on my flip-flops.

"It looks like there is an In-N-Out up there if that works for you?" He pointed up the road to a shopping center in the desert.

"That sounds good."

"Okay." He turned the music back up and hit scan to find a local channel. We exited the freeway and made a big loop until we were dropped on the road that led to our destination. The parking lot was completely full so we had to park in the back where the tour buses were all lined up. Groups of Japanese tourists were stretching their legs and carrying around various bags from the shopping center and food places nearby. It felt like a different world already even though we were only about halfway there.

The heat was dry and when the wind blew by, it felt like a blow-dryer directed right at my exposed skin. Usually I complained about the rise in temperature, but because we had wanted this trip so bad, the weather that day seemed like an adventure instead of a burden. We walked toward the door and Nolan's hand slipped into mine so casually it was clearly a product of our years of practice. I couldn't help swinging our hands between us and bouncing a little with the thrill of the day ahead of us. When we were kids we hated being stuck in the car for a long time, but now that this trip was born from our own imaginations, I finally understood how my mom had gazed out the window and was always talking about how beautiful everything was along the road. As a kid I wondered how brown dirt could be beautiful, but walking with Nolan miles from home made everything seem so much more vivid and alive. It was *all* beautiful.

We had to eat our lunch in his truck since there were no tables left inside. The shopping center was also on the way to Las Vegas, so bus after bus of tourists and retired people stopped and grabbed a bite to eat there. Other families stopped to let their dogs out or to use the restroom. We watched it all from inside the truck like it was a movie playing out right in front of us.

Nolan's truck thermometer said it was one hundred and twelve degrees when we crossed over the Colorado River and into the state of Arizona. A large white bridge stretched across what had once been only a thin blue line on Nolan's map. It was beautiful, a deep blue-green flowing between rocky shores, and I couldn't wait to stick my feet into the water. We still had about an hour left of our drive and the water disappeared again until we reached Lake Havasu City. Pulling into town was surreal as the lake stretched out before us, larger than I had even imagined.

We had decided we would eat out for most of our meals

but we still wanted to stop in town at a grocery store and buy some more snacks and drinks. Nolan had brought a small ice chest and we knew we'd need to fill it with ice and weren't sure if there was a place to do that in the condo building. We stopped at the Walmart right on the edge of town.

"Do you think you could ever live here?" I asked as he grabbed a hot cart that had been sitting in the parking lot.

"Right now I think yes, but a few days of this heat and I might change my mind." We were almost blown off our feet when the air-conditioning met us at the sliding doors. It was such a relief. We both took off our sunglasses and wiped the sweat from our cheeks before going any farther. It was fun shopping with him. We'd run errands for our parents and even for ourselves before, but being in a different state, on our own, made it feel like the first time. Even though we only needed a few things, we went up and down the aisles and had a little fun. I grabbed some new sunscreen and he tried on a few hats. Just when our bodies had adjusted to the cooler temperature, it was time to get back into the heat.

There was one main road into Lake Havasu from the direction we'd come and the farther we drove along it, the more the landscape around us seemed to develop until finally we found ourselves in the middle of the city. I was so impatient to see the bridge I practically bounced in my seat. The first time we missed the street we were supposed to be on and ended up going underneath where we wanted to be. The second time we made it and Nolan drove me over the bridge I'd had my heart set on seeing in person since that vacation so long ago. It didn't disappoint. Old gray blocks rose up ahead of us, the street on top lined with flags that were waving in the wind. Beneath, the channel flowed on both sides and I twisted my neck to take in everything I could all at once. It was over too quickly so we turned around in a shopping center parking lot and rode over it again.

Now that I'd seen the bridge from the top, I couldn't wait to stand beneath it or put my feet in the refreshing water I could see flowing below. We found the condo and retrieved the key before making a few trips to the truck to bring in everything. Our condo was on the first floor and was incredible. It had a kitchen, living room, and two bedrooms, each with their own bathroom. I immediately opened the big glass sliding door that opened from the living room and stepped out onto the patio where I could see the lake. A large gate separated the condo from the beach, but I could see the London Bridge in all her glory from our patio behind the black iron gate.

Nolan stepped out onto the patio with me, and I loved how big and infectious his smile was. I'd always thought I wanted to see the bridge and doing so would make me the happiest I could imagine. I had never really thought about seeing it with another person. Standing there in the heat of the desert with the most independence I'd ever been given, I realized I would have cheated myself if I didn't see the bridge with him. Experiencing things for myself was wonderful, but sharing that experience with someone I loved was really what made my world go round.

thirty

THE TWO OF us sat side by side in the lounge chairs the condo had in the front closet. Our feet were in the water that slowly lapped at the shore if a boat drove by, and since it was a weekend, there were lots of boats. I had wanted to walk to the bridge and see it up close, but it was so hot outside we figured it might be better to do after the sun went down. I was lying on my stomach to tan my back and was watching Nolan as he drifted off to sleep.

I could hear the light whoosh of the water as it crashed in the smallest wave and then receded back into the lake. There was not a cloud in the sky, and while we could hear music playing, it was as if the two of us were stranded on an island in paradise alone. Nolan picked his head up when he heard a boat grumble by and then he turned and gave me a smile before closing his eyes and resting again.

I wondered if he missed Erin. He hadn't talked about her since that day in his truck after Sasha had interviewed him, and I didn't want to bring it up if it was going to hurt him somehow. Erin and Nolan weren't talking anymore, but I wasn't sure if he had ended it or if she had. He didn't ask me about Jude either. In the days that had followed our secret coming out, it seemed like we both preferred to let our friendship fall back into the comfortable pattern it had been in before we ever let any lines be crossed. The only problem was that no matter how hard we might have wished we could, there was no undoing what had happened between us that night in the Jacuzzi.

Nolan cracked an eye open and turned toward me. "Why are you looking at me? Do you want to go in or something?" He sat up a little and rubbed his chest as he looked out at the boats slowly traversing the channel. I hadn't realized I'd been looking at him while in thought. "We should probably swim now if we're going to. Then later we can get out and walk down to the bridge to get some dinner."

I pushed myself up off the chair. We slowly stepped into the water, and once we were waist deep, we dropped low and let it cover our hot shoulders and backs. "Is it what you thought it would be?" he asked as we crouched in the refreshing water and stared down the channel to the London Bridge.

"It's pretty spectacular," I answered, moving my arms slowly to steer my body.

"When are you going to cross it off the list?" He turned to face me and we floated close together as the water moved around us in small swells.

"I almost don't want to," I answered honestly.

"Me either," he said, and then turned around again and watched a huge boat drive past us, its engine roaring and echoing through the shadows the bridge cast on the water. "We'll only have one thing left."

We stayed in the water until it was dark, reserved at first, just a couple of adults on a nice, mature vacation. Then we slipped back over that line we'd been walking and fell right into our childhoods, splashing around and laughing out loud, maybe even trying to drown each other. I never wanted to let go of that world with him. I decided as simply as the thought had crossed my mind that I'd be sure not to.

Once we dragged ourselves out of the lake and dried off, we realized just how hungry we were. We'd munched on some chips and drank water all day, but the sun seemed to zap all our energy and make us starving teens again during the night. We both took our showers and then decided to make the walk I'd been waiting for down to the bridge so I could see it up close and even touch it. He locked the door behind us and we took the pathway down to the sidewalk that wound with the channel and dipped under the bridge.

Nolan held my hand as we watched the sparrows building nests beneath the bridge. When we finally reached the big stone blocks, I ran my hand along them, wondering how many hands had touched that place before mine. Maybe even in London. We took a selfie and sent it to our parents and then walked beneath the huge arches and out the other side. Now when I played London Bridge with my children, I'd know what it really felt like to be near it.

On the other side of the bridge we found a pizza place. It was easy to do since the smell of freshly baked pizzas wafted down around us. We climbed up the steep hill that brought us to the top of the bridge where the pizza place was tucked near a fountain. We ordered our pizza and then moved out to the balcony that overlooked the bridge and the boats below it.

Nolan sat next to me and I propped my feet up on the iron fence that ran around the balcony. Even with all the heat around us, I could still feel him beside me. I wondered if I would always know exactly where he was when he was near and if his scent would be familiar to me even after we were no longer neighbors. Being Nolan's friend had been easy. Falling for him had been effortless. Maybe that kind of attraction would be fleeting, but as I sat there with him at my side, I knew that loving him was eternal.

"Do you ever think about your life in a few years?" he asked, staring out at the water, both of us avoiding eye contact.

"Yes. I've thought about it." I took a deep breath and let it out slowly, my chest tightening with anticipation.

"Well, what do you see?"

"I imagine I'll be in college. Hopefully finishing up a degree. I'll probably still be living close to home, but in an apartment or rental house with a roommate." It all seemed so fuzzy now, like my future was changing while we had the conversation.

"With who?" he asked, sounding like he already knew the answer. I thought hard about all of my friends. I tried to picture Nisha and me living together, but I knew that wasn't a great fit. Then I considered Regan, but that didn't feel right either. Maria? No.

"Can't picture it, can you?" he asked, squeezing my leg just a little so I'd look at him. He smiled at me but shook his head. "I can't either. I try to, I really do. I can imagine my bed and my dresser, the old poster of the trophy truck and even where I'd put my bulletin board or what snacks I'd keep in the fridge. I can imagine all that shit, but not a roommate."

I tried again to imagine it and could then see the little details he was talking about. I could picture the stark white walls of a new apartment and the purple and pink swirls of my favorite bedspread. I could imagine bringing with me the picture of him and me when we won first and second place in our bike rodeo in fifth grade. I'd set it on my desk. But in my head, when I stepped out of my room and into my imagined living room, the person I saw was him.

My ears were almost ringing with the peacefulness of the evening around us. We were alone on the balcony, three stories above anyone walking below. I turned to face him, trying so hard to bring my confession to the tip of my tongue. His eyes met mine and stayed locked with the most determined and tortured look I'd ever seen him wear. He grinned a little, and it made my heart hurt for a second because I could see his heart was heavy with a secret of his own. Just when I thought mine would burst through my lips, he whispered, "All I can ever see is you."

I drew in a breath right before his lips met mine and my world was lit on fire. His hand moved to the side of my face and his fingers slid into my hair, tipping my head slightly so he could deepen the kiss. I was falling—no, flying, soaring, but also diving. My heart was growing and expanding like the flame when the wick of a candle ignites. My eyes were closed but I could see him in my soul. His taste was familiar but his touch on my face felt so new. He pressed his lips to mine one last time and then pulled back far enough to really look at me. His gaze moved from my lips to my eyes as if he was searching for something. My chest heaved with a heavy breath, my head swimming—my body floating. He whispered, "Tell me you see me too."

thirty-one

"IT'S ALWAYS BEEN you," I said, and the burden of keeping that secret from him was lifted.

"The first time I kissed you, I thought I was doing the right thing," he said as he looked into my eyes. "I thought Jude made you happy, so I let you go so you could be with him."

I was already shaking my head. "I loved you."

"I didn't know. You told me not to tell Erin."

"I guess we wanted the same thing for each other," I said, reaching up to touch his face. "I thought she made you happy."

He shook his head gently and gave me a small kiss and then held my hand. "I've loved you for a long time. I first told my mom when I was nine. She told me she loved you too, but in my heart I knew it was different. She didn't need to be near you or know you were okay all the time." He brought my hand to his lips and kissed it. "I told her again when we were twelve. I told her, 'I love Zie,' and she told me she knew. I was braver then and said, 'No. I *love her*, love her.' She told me that being so close with someone felt good in your heart and that you and I were best friends." He chuckled a little and brought his free hand up to clasp on tighter to our joined ones.

"At fifteen I tried again. She was cooking dinner and it was just the two of us; my dad and brothers must have been at some event. I remember standing in that kitchen with her and saying, 'I love her, Mom.' I told her, 'It isn't the same love you have for her and it isn't just because she's my friend. I think I'm going to love her forever.'" He smiled at me and I thought my face was going to stay permanently frozen with the biggest smile I'd ever had until that joy overflowed within my heart and tears of happiness filled my eyes.

He cleared his throat and wiped a tear that escaped my eye with his thumb. "She told me I needed to be sure. She told me if I broke your heart I'd destroy what took years to build. I got scared. I wanted to protect you—not hurt you.

I decided if you ever wanted to fall in love with me I'd be there. I wouldn't ask to hold your heart unless you put it in my hands."

"I had no idea," I managed to whisper past the lump in my throat.

"I know," he laughed, swiping a strand of hair that had fallen in my face behind my ear. "I thought you would never see me as more than a friend."

"Don't be silly," I teased. "I fell in love with you first." Then I leaned in and kissed him because I finally could. I could love him in the open and give a voice to the words that had been trying to escape for years. The sound of a door swinging open and the bold smell of tomato sauce and cheese surrounded us. The young guy from behind the counter set our pizza on the table with a knowing grin.

Nolan grabbed my kit and handed it to me as he served our pizza. It was surreal to be sitting with him in that beautiful city under a bridge from a far land with nothing but honesty between us. "What about our parents?" I asked around a hot bite. He wiped his mouth before smiling.

"They'll still live next door to each other. Our moms will still get drunk before nine every month on game night and our dads will continue to pretend they don't enjoy it. They were friends before *us* and they'll be friends if ever there's an *after us*."

We finished up the pizza and walked hand in hand back down the big ramp. The bridge was lit up with bright lights strung together, and we stopped one more time to grab a picture. We stepped up to the wide column of blocks and I ran my fingers over them again. When Nolan held his arm out to center us on the screen of his phone, I moved in close to him, wrapping one arm around his waist. With our faces near but not touching, he snapped a picture and said, "This is before." His fingers swiped quickly over his screen, typing a message and sending the picture. I gave him a curious look, but he just pulled me back against him and smiled down on me with the camera out and our images centered perfectly. "And this is for after." He kissed me again and I heard the click of the camera go off.

"After what?" I asked when we broke apart.

"After that text that I just sent to everyone letting them know we are finally officially together." He turned his phone around so I could see the last picture of us kissing on the message screen. Our parents were very supportive of the news, but we were informed there would be new rules when we returned home from our trip.

The next morning, we woke up determined to finish our list before we had to leave the next day. We found a tattoo shop in town that could ink us both that day. I still had no idea what we were going to get when we walked into the colorful business, the bell above the door announcing our entrance.

"Welcome," the man behind the counter greeted us as he held out his hand for Nolan to shake. "How can I help you?"

"I called earlier," Nolan said, pulling me up to the counter by my hand. "We both want tattoos."

"Do you already know what you want?"

I looked at Nolan, curious if he'd already made a decision. I had been thinking about it since we first wrote the item on our list. Nothing seemed to make sense when I thought about having it on my body forever. Standing in the shop, Nolan seemed so confident. "I do."

It was perfect. I watched Nolan as the masculine text was inked onto his skin at his side, centered on his ribs. The single word would definitely be something he would be asked about forever.

Nolan checked out his tattoo in the mirror as the tattoo artist cleaned his station and prepped my ribs for the same permanent message. My script was tilted and feminine, but the word was the same. Nolan held my hand as I tried not to squirm when the needles danced across my skin. When it was finished, I stood in front of the mirror and read the word that would always remind us of this trip and the revelation that took traveling almost four hundred miles outside our boundaries to be brought to light.

"What does it mean to you guys?" the artist asked as he snapped his glove off his hand.

"It's a word that describes both our past and our future," Nolan answered, his eyes meeting mine in the mirror. "It's *always* been her, and it *always* will be."

That night when I pulled out my kit, I opened the pouch where I stored our list. I'd keep it forever, but I wanted to know what it felt like to put that final line through our last item and actually be happy about it. I unfolded it and ran my palm across the soft fibers to straighten it out. Beneath tattoos, another item had been written, and I let the tip of my finger slide over the letters pressed into the napkin in Nolan's writing. I used my pen to strike through the word *tattoos* and then folded the napkin and tucked it back where it belonged. After all, we had the rest of our lives to *always be best friends*.

Just as I was about to put my kit on the nightstand beside the bed, I saw that Nolan had left out a new sheet of paper and a pen. He'd already titled the list, but he'd only written two items, leaving some empty lines for me to fill in. I set my kit down and picked up the pen, smiling as I read TOP TEN

THINGS WE MUST COMPLETE AS COLLEGE FRESHMEN. I laughed as I read the first item and decided I'd wait until the end of summer to point out that security most likely frowned upon toilet-papering college mascots.

acknowledgments

When I was a teen I thought friendship was measured in volume. A therapist once told me that might be wrong. She suggested that as I grew older I'd come to understand my truest of friends would most likely be able to be counted on the fingers of my own hands. At the time I couldn't see that and sometimes longed to have a larger social circle. Lord knows I've been judged for my lack of one. I've always had a few close friends who have been there no matter what over the years. Our lives have come together and then grown apart as we each moved along our own journeys, only to come back again when we've found ourselves in some place where we needed to reach out. Recently I was the one picking up the phone. So this story—this book about life-long friends, falling in love, heartbreak, and wanting to be worthy—is the perfect place to thank my friends.

Jaime Angell, you have been unwavering in your support of me throughout this writing path I've chosen. You've picked up my pieces many times and are always the voice of reason I call when I need to be reassured and want someone who cares enough about me to be honest. You're always invested, no matter what is going on as you walk your own path, and for that I'll forever be grateful. Thank you.

Christina Zeller, the friend who taught me about the most amazing kind of tribe. The woman who refused to let a day go by without my phone buzzing during some hard times. I can't believe how lucky I was that the world saw fit to sit our wonderful little guys together so long ago. We might not be room moms anymore, but we are going to make excellent RAs at their college of choice. Not okay? Fine, at least I'll love my travel partner when we go to visit them. I can't thank you enough for everything.

Sandy Bruce, you are one strong woman. Your support and friendship helped more than you know. Sometimes I'm not sure I would have known which foot to put in front of the other without you. You were a peaceful calm, and if anyone has ever experienced chaos they will know how priceless that is. Thank you.

Lisa Miller and your basket of delicious cookies. You have always been there even when we haven't talked in ages. You are in little memories from so many moments of my life. I think of you as my kids discover old movies, songs from our youth, and when driving by our old favorite hangouts. Thank you for always being my friend.

Erika Altman, what a crazy ride we've been on since we first passed that note in that awful astrology class! I knew there was something about you that would make me want to know you forever. I'm so happy to call you my friend. Thanks for your support.

Melinda Di Lorenzo, you are an amazing author with a wicked talent for writing dialogue. You make me laugh and keep me motivated. You've given me not only hope in this career, but opportunities. You were so generous with your time to review this story and make sure it was true to life. You gave me perspective and insight. Thank you!

Elizabeth Chapman, thank you for sharing your knowledge about T1 and, of course, my wonderful niece. I love you.

Thank you to Catherine Wallace for supporting me and helping me share this book with the world. I will forever be grateful you gave me a chance at HarperTeen!

Thank you to my family for your support and understanding during the times I've had to work both jobs to make this happen. I love all of you very much. Love you Jake and Josh!!

And thank you to the readers who have been there with me since day one, and those who have found me along the way. I couldn't do this career without you. I hope you enjoyed the story!